Mysterious Martin
AND
For Art's Sake

Mysterious Martin

A Fiction Narrative Setting Forth
the Development of Character Along
Unusual Lines

AND

For Art's Sake

Tod Robbins

Introduction by Rebecca Peters-Golden

Hastings College Press | Hastings, Nebraska

Production Staff

Dakota Anderson

Emilie Barnes

Kaitlyn Baucom

Allie Belitz

Hannah Currey

Razvan Dobrin

Kaitlin Grode

Rachel Jesske

Alex Kreikemeier

Brooke MacLeod

Holly Wolfe

ISBN-10: 1942885083
ISBN-13: 978-1-942885-08-5

Note on the text: This edition has been reset from the first (1912, *Mysterious Martin*) edition and the revised (1920, "For Art's Sake") edition. Original spelling and grammatical conventions have been maintained, except in the case of publishing errors in the first editions. The original punctuation has been maintained but updated using modern conventions (e.g., eliminating spaces around dashes).

Contents

Introduction

The (Serial) Killer in Me Is the (Serial) Killer in You

Rebecca Peters-Golden

Notes on the text: Tod Robbins published three versions of the story you're reading. The first, *Mysterious Martin*, was published by J.S. Ogilvie Publishing Company in 1912; an expanded and revised version, "For Art's Sake," was included in Robbins' collection *Silent, White and Beautiful and Other Stories* in 1920; the final version, *The Master of Murder*, which is quite similar to "For Art's Sake," was published by Phillip Allan in 1933.

There are a number of superficial changes between the 1912 and 1920 versions: changes in location and character names, the introduction of a few new characters, and a shift in the timeline. The main way that "For Art's Sake" differs from *Mysterious Martin*, however, is that whereas in *Mysterious Martin* the crimes that Martin commits for the sake of his art are only confessed at the end, in "For Art's Sake," they come to light much earlier. Robbins adds a lengthy episode that implicates the narrator in these crimes, linking him with Martin and providing a lot more texture of the New York City demimonde. This, in turn, changes the ending of the 1920 version.

In this introduction I quote from both the 1912 and the 1920 versions of the novel, but for the sake of clarity, I'll consistently refer to the novel as *Mysterious Martin* and indicate which version I'm referring to in the citation.

Pulp Fiction and the Gothic

In Tod Robbins' 1918 story, "Silent, White and Beautiful," a sculptor murders four people and turns their bodies into art. It's a shocking conceit but of a type that's now familiar to us from horror movies and television shows. The shocking, the lurid, the grotesque, the titillating, and the downright weird … this was the world of the pulps—Tod Robbins' world.

Pulp magazines (the pulps), published from 1896 to the 1950s, were cheap, disposable fiction magazines with eye-catching covers that got their name from the wood pulp paper on which they were printed.[1] In a time of many popular monthly publications, the production quality of the pulps was bottom shelf, and its content was considered by many to be equally tawdry. The lifeblood of the pulps was sensational stories of adventure, horror, mystery, romance, and science fiction. They were sold cheaply to a mass market and paid authors less than traditional publications. For these reasons, even though authors such as Tennessee Williams, Jack London, Upton Sinclair, and Mark Twain published early works in the pulps, pulp fiction became a byword for all lurid, sensational, and lowbrow entertainment. There is a practical reason that the pulps embraced the style they did, though, with flashy plots, daring character choices, and playful hyperbole: in a glutted market, authors and magazines that became irrelevant—that failed to innovate, experiment, and titillate their audiences—would cease to be published, so they responded quickly and agilely to currents of modernity, crime, technology, and popular culture as they emerged.

While the pulps are only recently being included in the picture we paint of American literary modernism—that is, print

---

[1]   The acid that was needed to break the wood chips down to pulp made the paper extremely susceptible to deterioration. Their ephemeral quality contributed to the opinion that their content was as disposable as their paper. This also significantly prevented much of the material from entering into the literary canon, as it was erased from the record. For great information, statistics, and images, see The Pulp Magazines Project: www.pulpmags.org.

culture in the U.S. from about 1890 to 1950—their significance in general, and Robbins' in particular, can't be overstated, especially with regard to genre. As the market for the pulps increased throughout the 1910s and 1920s, they began to specialize by genre rather than combine stories of many genres in one publication. One magazine, that is, would devote itself to adventure stories, another to tales of love and romance, another to detective stories, and another to horror and science fiction. All of these genres were considered lowbrow, mass entertainment in contrast to literary fiction, which was read by a more elite audience and considered respectable art.

In practice, this distinction between the pulps and literary fiction was fuzzy at best; still, it's useful in picturing the literary landscape that viewed genre fiction as a different animal than the realist novel of the nineteenth century (e.g., *The Adventures of Huckleberry Finn* (1884) by Mark Twain) or the experimental modernist novel that was in the ascendant (e.g., *The Sound and the Fury* (1929) by William Faulkner). The distinctions among genres that resulted from the specialization of the pulps—science fiction, horror, romance, mystery, etc.—are ones that we still use to categorize fiction today, as we can see by wandering into any bookstore. Genre-wise, Tod Robbins' *Mysterious Martin* is a horror novel, with all the thrills, creep-outs, and spine-tingles of the short stories Robbins wrote for the pulps.

Mysterious Martin is the story of Sterling Martin, a brilliant, if sinister, painter and writer who insists that he has no imagination, but an incredible ability to put down the world exactly as he experiences it. This ability causes his tales of crime and murder to be widely admired. His second book, *The Confessions of Constantine*, written from the perspective of a murderer, is so powerfully descriptive that it causes the people who read it to become murderers themselves, and as a result, a crime wave sweeps New York that can be contained only by burning every copy of the book in print: "The police force fought valiantly to hold it in check, but failed. In vain they made countless arrests, for still new murderers sprang up on all sides.

It seemed as though it were a contagious disease, a murderer's microbe, as one learned fool maintained" (*Mysterious* 63).

When *Mysterious Martin* was first published in 1912, it was released into a literary climate that automatically associated all genre fiction with lowbrow, disposable entertainment for the masses. We can see this reflected in even the positive reviews of the novel. According to one surprised reviewer from *St. Joseph News Press*, it "is a book of horror, but is so well written and so cleverly conceived, that it should receive due credit." Another, from the *Albany Evening Journal*, writes that it is "so well done that one cannot condemn it because of the theme." This expectation that horror fiction would necessarily be poorly written and ill-conceived was a common impediment to taking genre fiction seriously or to including it in the literary canon.

It's useful, now, to give the pulps of Robbins' day some context by taking a look at their lineage, for they were really an extension of several different genres already in circulation. Pulp magazines became popular in America at the turn of the twentieth century and remained so until mid-century, when the post-war paper shortages combined with the increased popularity of comic books and television to chime the death knell of the pulps. The pulps were the direct descendants of the British penny dreadful and the American dime novel, both popular publications that, due to being inexpensive and sensational, appealed to a wide and varied readership. These, in turn, evolved from the gothic novel, the Newgate novel, and the sensation novel.

The genre of the criminal biography became hugely popular with the publication of the *Newgate Calendar* in Britain in the mid-eighteenth century (officially collected and published in 1774). This calendar contained short, sensational stories of Newgate prisoners' true crimes, accompanied by lurid woodcuts. In America, the *Newgate Calendar* was quickly echoed by *The American Bloody Register*, published in 1784. The Newgate novel, popular from the 1820s through the 1840s, grew out of the *Newgate Calendar*, expanding the stories of crime to novel-length and often glamorizing the lives and pursuits of the criminals.

Charles Dickens' *Oliver Twist* (1837) is considered a Newgate novel. The public's desire for sensational true crime was thus well-established when the penny dreadful began to be published in Britain in the 1830s, delivering thrills, chills, and often murder, for the price of one penny—far cheaper than reading Dickens. The penny dreadful was a weekly fiction magazine that frequently featured tales of famous criminals who would be familiar from the *Newgate Calendar* as well as rehashed versions of popular gothic novels.

In the 1840s and 1850s, a genre called the city mystery was all the rage in America and Europe. Best-selling city mysteries like George Lippard's exposé of Philadelphia, *The Quaker City* (1845), turn the city inside out, shining a bright light on the corruption, violence, and secrets that hide just beneath the surface of what we see. In America, dime novels were cheap paperbacks first published in the 1860s that began, like the penny dreadful, as reprints of previously published stories, but later transitioned to original material. As they were meant to appeal to a mass audience, westerns, mysteries, adventure stories, romance, and tales of urban crime were the norm, much like the pulps that would follow. In their heyday, dime novels were also rewritten for a British audience and published in the penny dreadfuls. At the turn of the twentieth century, changes in printing technology and the availability of cheap wood pulp paper found the pulp magazines gaining in popularity and the dime novel waning as many publishers switched formats.

There was a hunger for the sensationalism that had become central to literary production in America and Britain; it animated newspaper stories and novels just as it did the pulps. The 1860s and 1870s even saw the explosion of an entire genre called the sensation novel in Britain, which was also based on the Newgate novel. Sensation novels featured shocking subjects such as murder, insanity, adultery, and seduction. Sensation novels combined the journalistic realism of true crime with the disturbing horror of the gothic to portray familiar settings as threatening. This undermined the middle-class assumption that sensational and violent occurrences were separate from their homes. This was an assumption that came, in part, from the gothic novel, where the settings of terror and horror are not the familiar domestic spaces of the middle-class home, but crumbling castles in far-flung locales.

Let's turn to those gothic novels now, because they are the lightning strike from which so many of the genres that influence the pulps emanate. But, more than that, I want to think of the public reception of the gothic as something with which *Mysterious Martin* is in direct conversation. There are many subgenres of the gothic novel, which became popular in the 1780s and 1790s, but what they all share is that their sensationalism is intended to produce strong affective responses in the reader. By the time the gothic novel exploded onto the scene in Britain, the novel-reading public was largely female, and, due to the rise in literacy, was no longer limited to the aristocracy. The market for the gothic novel, then, was huge, and, due to its mass readership, there was widespread concern about the power that the gothic novel might exert over these female readers. It's useful to note that novels in general were seen as potentially socially subversive because they created realistic worlds for the reader to enter and characters for the reader to identify with. In contrast to the satires or epics that preceded them, these novels presented the danger that readers might become so engrossed in their worlds that they could believe them to be true.

The gothic—a genre that combined the form of the novel with the shock of horror—was, therefore, considered particularly problematic. Add to this the element of romance often found in gothic novels and they were seen as fomenting a dangerously intimate relationship with the reader, infecting her with strong feelings and, potentially, desires that were considered inappropriate for a lady of the time. Further, many critics feared that entering this realm of identification and sensation would cause (particularly female) readers to lose touch with reality altogether. The massive popularity of the gothic, then, made this fear of the power of sensation in fiction a well-known anxiety of the period.

Indeed, the central anxiety of *Mysterious Martin* is the same one that animated critique of the gothic novel: can art have power over us? Of course, concern over the power of art or rhetoric to affect, say, the public's political sympathies, has been a feature of the critical response to art as far back as Plato's *Republic* (around 380 BCE). But, as I detailed above, there was intense suspicion that reading gothic novels could have a particularly dangerous effect. The public fear of reading gothic novels, however, cannot hold a candle to the effects of reading Sterling Martin's books in *Mysterious Martin*.

Sterling Martin's *The Confessions of Constantine*, as I mentioned, renders a murder so vividly and skillfully that it induces those who read it to feel like—and then become—murderers themselves. "You, my readers," the narrator says, "know those terrible sensations with which [the book] inspired you" (*Mysterious* 62). One reviewer of Martin's novel writes, "my hand was steady as I turned the pages, but in my brain was forming the blood lust of the murderer as he struck the fatal blow. I felt no repulsion at the savagery of it, but only the great unholy joy of brute rage and the love of killing" (*Mysterious* 62). *Mysterious Martin*, that is, demonstrates precisely the power of art that detractors of the gothic novel so feared.

Mysterious Martin, further, owes much to Edgar Allan Poe, who was part of Dark Romanticism, the name given to the fiction of Nathaniel Hawthorne, Washington Irving, Herman Melville, and, of course, Poe, in America, where the heyday of the gothic was the nineteenth century. These works are gothic stories that, in contrast to pulp ephemera, were considered to have literary value even while they touched on sensational subjects. Poe's stories of murder, incest, live burial, torture, and madness often hearkened back to an earlier era, but were considered so affecting because they tapped into modern cultural and psychological anxieties.[2]

---

[2]   Further, the publication of Poe's "The Murders in the Rue Morgue" in 1841 is often cited as the beginning of the genre of detective fiction as we conceive of it today. He wrote two others: "The Mystery of Marie Rogêt" (1842) and "The Purloined Letter" (1844). Critics will argue that we can locate seeds of detective fiction as early as the Bible, but with "The Murders in the Rue Morgue"

In *Mysterious Martin* a reviewer of Sterling Martin's earlier work writes, "I think that Martin's 'Many Murders' contains the greatest piece of horror writing since the days of Poe, and in my opinion indeed even that gifted genius had not the realistic touch that makes 'Many Murders' a masterpiece of the terrible" (*Mysterious* 48). And, "Not since the days of Poe has America produced such a consummate craftsman. I do not hesitate to say that even the immortal creator of 'The Gold Bug' had not the power of description which makes ... Martin's work unforgettable" ("For Art's Sake" 173). It is notable that Robbins chose Edgar Allan Poe's work to compare Martin's to. Robbins' invocation of Poe, the landmark of the American gothic, in association with an author who has the power to infect readers with the compulsion to murder further draws our attention to the lineage of anxiety about gothic novel readers. *Mysterious Martin* dramatizes this critique—with a bit of a wink, I believe—by demonstrating that such detractors were right: books *do* have the power to overcome us and books with a mass readership *do* have the potential to quickly infect the entire reading population.[3]

Regionalism and *Mysterious Martin*

The importance of publishing regional texts is to challenge ideas about what the landscape of the canon of American literature looks like. Since, so often, the texts that fall out of print are those that describe minority experiences—the experiences of rural folks, queer experiences, experiences of people of color, etc.—it is crucial to make those texts available again because by

---

Poe certainly crystallizes the tropes of the genre. Poe's detective, C. Auguste Dupin, is the prototype of Arthur Conan Doyle's Sherlock Holmes and Agatha Christie's Hercule Poirot, to cite the most famous examples.

[3]   This element of *Mysterious Martin* is also a poignant callback to what is considered the first American gothic novel, Charles Brockden Brown's *Wieland: or, The Transformation: An American Tale* (1798), in which a character throws his voice to make a man thinks he's being given divine instructions to murder his family.

doing so we reintroduce those voices and those experiences into the stories we tell about America and American literature.

Given this, it may seem counterintuitive to include a book like *Mysterious Martin* in a series of forgotten regional texts: after all, it's a book set mainly in Paris and New York City; a book about well-to-do white men; a book about urban artists. There are two ways in which *Mysterious Martin* can be seen as a regional text, however. Not only do the events of the novel have rippling effects on the rural spaces of the American landscape, but the novel also recognizes New York City as a regional space.

While published in 1912, *Mysterious Martin* begins in the early 1860s—"It was a beautiful spring day, some fifty years ago, that Martin first came into my life" (*Mysterious* 5); that is, it begins during the American Civil War. By "For Art's Sake," then, published in 1920, the story would have begun during the era of Reconstruction. Robbins uses the crime wave that sweeps the United States after the publication of Martin's second novel to highlight the tenuous state of fraught race relations in the South:

> But perhaps the Southern States suffered most of all. Of late years lynching parties had been rather few and far between; now they happened again with almost machinelike regularity. Scarcely a day passed in any of those towns on the other side of the Mason and Dixon's line when some negro did not dance out his life at the end of a rope. And the leaders of these lynching parties—the men who adjusted the noose about the cowering wretch's neck or lit the fagots which had been piled up against his knees— were invariably men of keen sensibilities and higher education—men who would have shrunk from such a task a few months before." ("For Art's Sake" 210)[4]

---

[4] In the 1920 version of the story, Robbins also shifts the end of the novel from rural North to rural South: Maine to Florida.

The murder spree that affects the southern states, therefore, is not a result of just southern politics. Robbins' revision of *Mysterious Martin* links the racist actions of the Reconstruction-era South directly to the urban space of New York City. The traditional distinction between urban and rural spaces is thus broken down, and the blame for such actions is distributed more equitably across the United States.

Another reason that it's important to have a diversity of regionalist texts available to us, though, is that their presence allows us see the range of experiences *within* any one place. This diversity allows us to dig beneath the surface and map the terrain hidden there. We can think of this as a kind of depth model of regionalism, and it is particularly useful in thinking about urban texts, since urban spaces aren't often read in regionalist terms. The New York City of, say, Edith Wharton's *The House of Mirth* (1905) doesn't encourage regionalist reading since it largely conforms to the dominant picture of gilded age urban wealth. *How the Other Half Lives: Studies Among the Tenements of New York* (1890), a work of photojournalism by Jacob Riis that documents the atrocious living conditions of poor and immigrant workers, though, is absolutely a work of urban regionalism. It looks at New York City not as a monolithic urban backdrop but as a patchwork of discreet, though interconnected, neighborhood spaces, each of which possesses its own characteristics.

Tod Robbins approaches the space of New York City from the perspective of a horror writer. Horror is a genre that takes familiar places and flips them inside out. That is, Robbins shows us a city that might look familiar on the surface, but he lifts the veil to show us its dark, gothic underbelly. Thinking about *Mysterious Martin* as a regionalist text opens up an important conversation about how genre and regionalism are related in literature and popular culture. For example, it allows us to complicate our discussion of the xenophobia in H.P. Lovecraft's horror stories set in New York City—"He" (1926) and "The Horror at Red Hook" (1927)—with questions of regionalism as well as those of ethnicity and class. Further, it raises questions like: Why are rural populations so often portrayed as monsters *because of* their rurality in horror films like *Texas Chainsaw Massacre* (1974) and *The Hills Have Eyes* (1977)?

Finally, *Mysterious Martin* dramatizes the ways that we are trained to map certain traits onto certain environments, or regions. Robbins shows us a character in possession of traits that we usually associate with non-regional urban texts—privilege, money, education, connections—and then he places this character in unfamiliar gothic spaces. This recontextualization demonstrates the creeping unease that is produced when a character who might seem to fit in Edith Wharton's New York City turns out to dwell in a much darker place.

The Serial Killer in Popular Culture

But there is another story about genre that *Mysterious Martin* helps us tell. *Mysterious Martin* can also be read as an entry in a subgenre that, while prevalent in popular culture today, has a rather thready genealogy …

When the popularity of the gothic novel was at its height in Britain, from the 1780s to the 1830s (known as the Romantic period), the figure of the genius was central to notions of artistic production. The genius was a man (for he was always a man) of great inspiration and creativity who produced original work from his imagination. He was sometimes tortured, sometimes emotional, and always in the grips of artistic fervor.

Like the romanticized figure of the artistic genius, Sterling Martin goes to great lengths for his craft, committing murder to fuel his art. His goal is to write the stories that he believes will appeal to the widest audience. "An accident happens on the street," he says. "In a moment hundreds have collected, drawn by the curious love for the terrible, a human trait. In my stories, that same throbbing sensation of horror will be ever present. People will buy them by the thousands, and going home to comforts and safety, experience the delightful feeling of tragedy by their own firesides" (*Mysterious* 35). Martin claims that he cannot innovate, but only replicate what he experiences. Fortunately for Martin, he is an expert at replication, both in his painting and in his writing, and is immediately lauded as a genius at both. In order to create the throbbing sensations of horror that are his goal, though, Martin must murder, and, to do so, he must kill any part of himself that would feel guilt over the murder: "For many months," Martin explains, "I trained myself for the career I had chosen, killing off my human virtues one by one, and thus gradually molding myself into a heartless machine" (*Mysterious* 91).

In short, Martin, whose skill is in his ability to replicate the details of reality but not to innovate, is the inverse of the Romantic genius. A heartless killing machine and an artistic genius would seem to be opposed. This combination, however, animates a whole strain of postmodern novels, of which *Mysterious Martin* can be read as an important prototype: the subgenre that we now call serial killer narratives.

It's useful to understand that the contemporary subgenre that we can coherently call the serial killer narrative started as a trickle in the 1950s, with a few standout examples drawing the public's attention to its presence, and then gradually rose during the 1970s and 1980s until it became the very visible presence in popular culture that it is today. Of course, there were books about multiple murderers before the second half of the twentieth century (like *Mysterious Martin*), but the term "serial killer" didn't make its way into wider culture until 1981, when *The New York Times* used it to describe serial killer Wayne Williams. The term comes not from fiction, but from law enforcement. It began to appear in the United States in the late 1960s and early 1970s and is variously attributed to law enforcement officers and, most famously, Robert Ressler, an FBI profiler. Though the word for serial murderer can first be found in a 1930 article in German, it really isn't until the 1970s that we can begin thinking in terms of a genre or subgenre of narratives.

The few serial killer narratives published in the 1950s were, at the time, considered to be in the genre of crime fiction. Crime and hardboiled detective novels were, of course, an offshoot of the pulps that became popular at midcentury when the pulps' popularity declined. Jim Thompson's 1952 novel *The*

Killer Inside Me, which tells the story of a small-town deputy
sheriff who is also a sadistic murderer, never uses the term
"serial killer," of course. It's written in the first-person from the
murderer's perspective. Soon after, Patricia Highsmith published
The Talented Mr. Ripley (1955), the first of five Ripley novels.
More pulpy still, Robert Bloch's *Psycho* (1959), is loosely based
on the habits of real-life serial killer Ed Gein and gained huge
popularity when Alfred Hitchcock adapted it for film a year
later.

The genre took a turn toward the non-fictional in the next
decades, and the spark that lit the postmodern bonfire of true
crime was Truman Capote's *In Cold Blood* (1966). It takes a
novelistic approach—Capote called it a "non-fiction novel"—to
the real-life 1959 slaying of the Clutters, a family in a small
town in Kansas. It was widely lauded as the greatest work
of true crime ever written, its sensational subject matter no
impediment to its praise. The same cannot be said of the many
non-fictional accounts of serial killers that it inspired. The most
notable examples include Vincent Bugliosi and Curt Gentry's
Helter Skelter: The True Story of the Manson Murders (1974);
Ann Rule's *The Stranger Beside Me* (1980), about serial killer
Ted Bundy; Robert Graysmith's *Zodiac* (1986), chronicling the
murders of the Zodiac killer; and Michael Newton's *Waste Land*
(1998), about the Charles Starkweather and Caril Ann Fugate
murders. Unlike *In Cold Blood*, these, and books like them, are
nearly always characterized as pulp entertainment due to their
subject matter, their sensationalism, and their merely serviceable
prose.

But let's get back to Tod Robbins. We can certainly see
the inspiration of the Newgate novels and penny dreadfuls in
Mysterious Martin's sensationalism, but in those, the ne'er-do-
wells, though glamorized, are nearly always lower-class brigands
whose criminality is laid at the feet of society's failures. The
middle-class reader might admire their outlawry but would never
wish to occupy their position. Martin, on the contrary, is urbane,
respectable, and privileged: he is educated at Yale and studies
in Paris, and he has money and connections. When he enters

the demimonde to kill for his art he is definitely slumming. As such, Martin owes much of his pedigree to the gentleman villains who came before him: dashing aristocratic figures who possess qualities that the reader might admire rather than admonish—outwardly, at least (think Count Dracula dressed for dinner rather than Frankenstein's creature in rags). Further, Martin's writing in *The Confessions of Constantine*, the novel that causes a wave of murders, specifically targets educated readers like himself:

> Strange to say … these modern murderers sprang, not from the illiterate, uneducated classes, as one might fancy, but from the reading public and more especially from the highest intellectual types.… As this crimson wave passed over the country, leaving horror and desolation in its track, the creative thinkers, who had as yet remained untouched, began to ask themselves a multitude of questions: What would be the final outcome of this catastrophe? If the higher type of intelligence fell victim to this homicidal mania, what could one expect from the illiterate, unimaginative masses who were born to follow like so many sheep? For the first time in human history, education had joined hands with crime. ("For Art's Sake" 210)

As a privileged, upper class murderer who kills for his art—art that is considered ingenious—Martin is something of a transitional character between the Romantic gentleman villains that preceded him and the postmodern pop culture serial killers that are to come. As we move into these more recent fictional serial killer narratives—film and television currently being the most influential—it is important to note that the serial killers of pop culture are framed quite differently from the real-life serial killers that have been studied and profiled by the FBI. This may seem obvious, since it is fiction, after all, but the deviations from reality that the subgenre takes are quite telling.

I've been discussing the historical figure of the genius because genius has been the most significant deviation from real-life serial killers in the pop cultural imagination. It is worth noting that real-life serial killers have not been shown to possess such genius; rather, they tend toward average intelligence.[5] While Martin's genius is that he's an artist himself, the contemporary figure of the serial killer in popular culture is often an intellectual genius. He still has a relationship with art, but it is often in the realm of aesthetic appreciation. That is to say, he is brilliant, educated, intellectual, and a connoisseur of highbrow culture; he hews to what we might broadly call good taste. This good taste is something of a joke in the most iconic contemporary serial killer figure, Dr. Hannibal Lecter, from Thomas Harris' 1988 novel *The Silence of the Lambs*. Lecter is a brilliant psychiatrist, sophisticate, and cannibal killer who always pairs the right wine with his human meals. In Hannibal Lecter and the many contemporary characters that he inspires, the figure of the serial killer and the figure of the genius have merged.

Keeping this in mind, let's return to Martin's murders. "What is one human life more or less?" Martin asks the narrator after one murder. "They are like ants, such men—only not so industrious. This fellow perished to-night in a good cause—for art's sake, indeed, for I intend to make the description of his murder a masterpiece" ("For Art's Sake" 158-159). To this, the narrator responds, "You're not human, Martin" ("For Art's Sake" 159). Martin values art more than he values human life. This quality is a crucial characteristic of the contemporary figure of the genius serial killer. He is someone for whom art and aesthetics are the highest calling. The elevation of art over life seems monstrous—inhuman—because it is devoid of empathy. It takes art, which we think of as being an essentially human pursuit, and uncouples it from humanism.

For Hannibal Lecter, manners and good taste are the most important things, and he often kills and consumes those in whom he finds them lacking. Lecter possesses all the trappings of the cultured upper class—his highbrow taste in classical music,

---

[5]   For more on real-life serial killers and their FBI profiles, see Robert Ressler's *Whoever Fights Monsters: My Twenty Years Tracking Serial Killers for the FBI* (1992).

art, and literature, his knowledge of philosophy, and, of course, his profession. These are all qualities that we associate with gentility and, therefore, safety, so they cloak him from suspicion, making him even more dangerous. This figure is remarkable because the same qualities that make him seem refined also serve to make us sympathetic to his crimes. That is, we would rather identify with a brilliant aesthete (even if he is a murderer) than with his victims, who fail to meet his criteria of education, taste, and manners.

Still, though we admire Lecter and wish to identify with him rather than against him, he is still a villain, a threat. By the turn of this century, however, characters who aestheticize serial murder are all over popular media. And, now, it is common for the serial killer to be the *hero*. In television shows such as *Dexter* (2006–2013), based on Jeff Lindsay's novel *Darkly Dreaming Dexter* (2004), the serial killer is the protagonist and we cross our fingers that he won't get caught. Dexter is framed as a "good" serial killer because he has turned his impulse to kill in a positive direction, killing only other killers. Like Lecter, he aestheticizes murder, reveling in victims' blood—he's a forensic blood spatter pattern analyst—and, at the beginning of the series, relishing what he considers a particularly brilliant murder artist who drains his victims' blood, dismembers them, and wraps some of their pieces in paper and string. In the television show, these scenes of murder look more like a modern art installation than a crime.

And, really, this figure of the aestheticized genius serial killer has, by 2015, become such a standby of the subgenre that it's fairly hackneyed. But, of course, that is an element of genre itself: the characteristics that make it recognizable eventually become repeated so often that they lose their power and become clichés. Like *Dexter, Hannibal,* a television show based, again, on Hannibal Lecter, presents us with scene after scene of murder victims meticulously arranged to appear beautiful: murder as art, just as Martin viewed it.

It is clear, I think, how prescient *Mysterious Martin* was in predicting a direction in which popular fiction would go.

Martin, though certainly not the first to suggest that humans are mesmerized by stories of murder, certainly had our number. If he could see us sitting on our couches and mainlining media chock-a-block with murder, I don't think he'd be a bit surprised.

....

Rebecca Peters-Golden is a writer living in Philadelphia. She received her PhD in English in 2011 from Indiana University, where she spent her time throwing elaborate themed dinner parties when she wasn't busy writing about the genre she calls "gothic realism." Her academic work explores the political and social resonances of genre, seriality, and modernity in the American novel. Now she writes fiction and poetry, and writes about food and literature for the online food magazine *Good. Food. Stories.* She also works as a freelance editor and recipe tester. One time, she won a chili cook-off.

Mysterious Martin

Introduction

It is scarcely a wise thing to pry too closely into the secrets of the dead, and especially should the graves of genius be respected by the mob, but I believe, in this case, the world should know the truth. Indeed, Martin himself, when almost at his last gasp, said as much, and expressed the wish that I hold nothing back.

I am an old man as I write these words, yet my mind, thank God! is still young, and my memory undimmed by years. The work that Martin accomplished will stand a monument to him long after my bones are crumbling, yet I do not envy him in the least, for his mind was ever a twisted, crooked thing, that made his life, and that of many others about him, a hell on this earth.

But now that he is dead, may he rest in peace.

I

Till the world goes down to rest
Men hold strength for all time blest.

It was a beautiful spring day, some fifty years ago,
that Martin first came into my life. I was a senior in Yale
at the time, rooming with my younger brother who had
just entered college. From my four years' experience in
university ways, I attempted to form his career by moral
precept and example, but from the first I had my hands full,
for the boy, even at that time, had a strong taste for drink.
He was a favorite with all, however, for his child-like sunny
disposition, and his handsome boyish face made up for his
occasional backslidings. After one of his sprees, and this is
a strange thing, his actions would puzzle and worry me. He
would be an entirely changed man for the space of several
hours, wrapt up in gloomy reflections and remorse. At those
times the slightest word of reproach would well-nigh drive

him mad, and we had to treat him like a child, tell him stories, or resort to anything to get his mind off himself.

On this bright day I was sitting beside the open window with a book before my eyes, studying for the examinations soon to come, and wishing heartily that I could be out under the trees with the fellows, whose voices I could hear through the casement.

Suddenly my door was thrown open, without the ceremony of a knock, and my brother's smiling face appeared in the aperture.

"Hello, Charley!" he cried. "Still grinding, I see," and then, not waiting for a response, he went on in his usual light-hearted way. "Such a bully time last night. The whole class was there. Got a little tight, and didn't want to come home. Knew you'd make me as blue as a corpse with your advice to the prodigal. No hard feelings, old chap?" and he held out his hand boyishly.

I had been worried about his not showing up the night before, and was prepared to give him a piece of my mind, but his frankness won me over, as it always did, and so I grasped his hand and shook it warmly.

"That's all right, Paul," I said. "But where did you spend the night?"

"Oh, a chap by the name of Martin took me under his wing," he answered readily. "Don't suppose you know him, as he keeps himself very much to himself; but he's a fine fellow, and can tell a funny story some. He told me one this morning that brought me out of my blues in no time."

"What is he, a freshman?" I asked a little condescendingly.

"Yes," said Paul; "but quite out of the ordinary. Martin is going to Paris to study art next year, so I asked him

around to meet you. Thought you might hit it off, and
room together over there. Here he is now," and he jumped
to his feet, as a tall, slender young man entered.

I was prepared to meet the usual loud, boyish freshman,
and was armed with all the senior's haughty condescension
for the encounter, but the man who entered my door, and
incidentally my life, took all the wind out of my sails on the
instant.

He seemed to create an atmosphere of his own,
a kind of power, and yet beside this, something more,
and somehow far deeper. As I rose to shake his hand, I
experienced this second and deeper feeling to the uttermost.

It is hard to describe, in fact, almost impossible, and
the nearest thing I can think of, only touches it slightly.
I felt then as though I had a secret, and he was trying to
draw it out of me against my will. All the dull anger and
suspicions of such a feeling were mine but for a moment,
for no sooner had I touched his cold hand than they
vanished completely. This, I learned later, was a common
experience of all those who met this strange man.

As I have said, he was very tall and thin, and yet he
had a certain catlike agility about him, at great variance
with his sallow skin and sunken body. His eyes were small
and gray, and they shifted continually from one object to
another, yet they impressed me that could they be focused
on a thing for any length of time they could bore into that
thing like gimlets.

Martin sank into a morris chair with unconscious
grace, and we were soon discussing the usual college topics.
I say we, meaning Paul and myself, for our visitor kept a
disconcerting silence. Finally Paul, thinking him no doubt
diffident in the presence of a respected senior, spoke up:

"Say, Martin," he said, "tell us that story you gave me this morning. It sure was good."

The man nodded in assent, and straightway began. Now the thing was humorous in itself, but he told it in a way to make a grave-digger laugh. Paul and I were convulsed in merriment to the point of tears when he had done, but he had never changed the blank expression on his face, although once I thought I saw his lip rise in the faintest suggestion of a sneer.

"Good heavens, man," I cried, as soon as I got my breath back, "with the talent for telling a story like that, you ought to be on the stage. Do you study English under Dr. Johnstone?"

"What makes you ask that?" said he.

"Your wording was so perfect," I replied. "It was as though the story were a machine, and every word that you used a perfect part of it that fitted exactly into its place. I don't think you could either add a word, or remove a word, without weakening the story somewhat."

"And you think that old conventional fool, with his parrot-learned knowledge, could teach me to do that?" cried Martin in sudden heat. "Why, I could teach him."

I had felt the man's power by now, but I also experienced a strange irritation at his words. Genius is a hard thing to put up with in others, so I replied rather tartly that I had my doubts of that, as Johnstone was a pretty good man in his line.

He smiled for the first time that day. "Maybe you are right," said he in a tone that he might have used to a child; "but English is beside the question. I came here to talk to you of art. I am going to Paris next year, and I heard that you were also. Am I right?"

"Yes," I said, "I am going to study under Julien."

"And so am I!" cried Martin. "We could room together over there. What do you think of it?"

"A fine idea," I replied half-heartedly, for the thought of living with such an insufferable egotist as I deemed him then was not alluring.

"That's settled then," said our guest as he rose to take his departure. "Come over and see me. Paul knows the way, and I am home every night," then he was gone down the passageway.

"Well, what do you think of him?" asked my brother a few minutes later.

"I don't know! Give me your opinion, Paul," I said.

"I think," replied the boy, "that he is going to be a great man—a very great man."

"He is already a great egotist," cried I, and opened my discarded book once more.

II

How different are the thoughts of men,
As jotted down by the writer's pen.
Some seem to have reflected the sky's blue,
While others the clouds' darker hue.

In spite of a determination I had formed not to visit Martin, the entreaties of Paul, and, to tell the truth, the curiosity with which the man inspired me, weakened my resolve.

On the very next evening, therefore, I set out through the streets of New Haven to look him up. Paul went with me as guide, and enlivened the way with a continual stream of disconnected ideas, in his usual light-hearted fashion.

"You will see, the place is a regular hermit's cave," he whispered as we knocked on the door.

Sure enough, when we were admitted by our host, the bareness of the interior was the first thing I noticed. The room appeared to be unusually large, but this impression was gathered through the absence of all furniture, with the exception of three old rickety chairs in a corner. Even the walls were unadorned by pictures and the usual trimmings of a college room. This man must be very poor, I thought, and it is to be owned, at that moment, the idea of rooming with him in Paris faded away completely.

"You find it unattractive from an artist's standpoint?" asked Martin. His roving gray eyes were for the once fixed upon me.

"No—that is, I mean yes. It is rather bare, don't you think," I stammered, like a schoolboy caught in a fault.

"Exactly," he responded quickly; "and therefore the abode of an artist."

"But I don't get your point," I broke in. "Why should an artist live, you'll excuse me, without the comforts of life?"

"Because," he answered, "an artist must be a man apart with no human weaknesses or desires. In other words, love of luxury and ease blights genius in the bud."

"How so?" I asked in surprise.

"Merely that luxury and ease can mean but one thing," he went on, "and that thing is the spending of money. You ask what does the money mean? I tell you it means the degrading of art to the dollar sign, and the prostitution of genius. We then become no longer superior men, but sink to the position of the organ-grinder's monkey that is pelted with pennies. He amuses the mob with his grotesque antics, and so do we. It may be that the world does not know this, but we know it, and that's what hurts. I would rather eat bread and cheese the rest of my life, and do the work that is in me, than take all that the world can offer, and be a living lie."

He spoke with his usual cold deliberation, but there was a bright red spot in either cheek, and a light in his eyes, that did not tally with his seeming calm.

"What special work do you intend taking up?" he asked me suddenly.

"Portrait painting," I answered.

"Then," he said, "you should have the tastes of a Spartan," and turning on his heel he left us, still standing in the middle of the room, while he opened a closet in a corner.

Evidently, I thought, conventionalities are nothing to him, but I wondered what he meant by that last remark of his.

He took something out of the dark recess, something flat and square, covered by a black cloth, and placed it on a shelf, in the best light that the gloomy room afforded.

"I want you to criticise this," cried Martin, and he drew off the covering with the deft motion of a conjurer.

I gasped in sheer wonderment at what I saw. To my as yet untrained eye, it was the most remarkable painting that I had ever beheld, and it affected me strangely. Although it was intensely warm in the place, I felt cold shivers run up my spine, and a feeling of deathly nausea crept over me, as I invariably experience in the presence of a corpse.

The painting that affected me thus was horribly lifelike, or, rather, deathlike. A young girl, lying dead on a road blocked with snow, seemed, if you can understand me, to be a real girl, and the road, with its sleigh-tracks, a real road, but last of all, the red blood from the white neck seemed to be slowly sinking into the snow as you watched, and reddening it.

"Why, Martin," I cried, "this is the work of a great artist. You don't mean to tell me that it is yours?"

"Yes," he answered slowly, "it is mine sure enough; but it is very crude," he finished, "and won't do."

"Crude?" I shouted. "Why the thing is a masterpiece, and fairly stands out of the canvas. You're too modest, that's the trouble with you."

"Modest? Nothing of the sort," he retorted with irritation. "Nobody is, and only fools pretend to be. If I thought it was really first class I wouldn't go to Paris, but I know I need a few little touches."

"Where did you get the idea?" I asked, ignoring what he had just said.

"I found her that way myself," he explained. "She was a friend of mine, and so it was a bit tough on me at first, but I realized what an excellent model she made, and so I sat down in the snow, and made a rough sketch of her just as she was."

"Murdered?" I asked. "Who murdered her?"

"Yes," chimed in Paul in unusual excitement, "who did murder her? I hope they caught the dog and strung him up."

"No, the murderer was never found," said Martin slowly, "and never will be now, I imagine."

"And you mean to say," broke in Paul, "that you sat down in cold blood and drew her as she lay there bleeding. That's a good one, that is. Isn't he a would-be hard-hearted brute, Charley? Why, I bet he beat his own shadow back to town."

Martin regarded him with a kind of cold curiosity in his eyes.

"I see that you are a character reader," he said with the faintest suggestion of a smile.

"Not at all," answered Paul; "but no one, with human blood in their veins, could come upon a murdered friend, and then sit down and make, a sketch of it. Why the thing is impossible."

"Maybe you are right," agreed Martin; "but, at any rate, that is exactly as she looked when I found her."

"She was exceptionally pretty then?" cried I. "What was the motive of the crime?"

"Absolutely none," replied our host, with a shrug of his shoulders; "or, at least, none that could be discovered. But let's say no more about it, for it's a nasty story and brings up unpleasant recollections." So saying, he covered the picture with the black cloth, and returned it to the closet.

"Do you know," said Paul with a forced laugh, "I feel much more comfortable with that thing out of the way. It fairly gave me the creeps."

"Thank you," said Martin gravely. "That is a genuine compliment."

We seated ourselves, and the talk drifted into other channels. Martin gave us a glimpse into his boyhood days, and a strange, gloomy childhood it was.

At an early age he had lost both father and mother in a railroad accident, and then a half-demented great-aunt had taken him to live with her in a lonely house way out in the country. Here, shut off from all companionship with other children, he grew to manhood. Luckily for him, the house had at least a good-sized library, composed for the most part of the classics, and these he read and mastered from cover to cover.

His aunt had many peculiarities. She was a firm believer in spiritualism, and considered herself a medium between this world and the other. Once Martin told us she had him sent to her room, where she asked him if he wanted to talk with his dead parents. He said no in fear and trembling, whereupon she had gone into a kind of fit, tearing her hair and foaming at the mouth. Just as the little child was well-nigh swooning from fright, she came to herself again, and told him that because he had refused to speak to the spirits of his parents, they had nearly torn her soul away in anger.

"Never, never do it again!" she screamed after him as he left the room.

Therefore, whenever he was sent for again, and it was many times, he always replied in the affirmative. Then the lights were put out, and he asked his dead parents whatever questions he wanted to, and a strange, sepulchral voice would answer.

"Of course, it was my aunt all the time," he concluded; "but I didn't know it, and my teeth would click together like castanets. When you consider that I was a child of five or six at the time, you can readily understand the effect it had on my forming mind."

"What became of your aunt?" I ventured.

"She died at last," he replied with a laugh, "and went to join her spirit friends, I fancy, but long before that I knew the whole thing to be a farce. Tell me," he changed the subject quickly, "you thought I was very poor when you first came in, didn't you?"

"Yes," I acknowledged, reddening; "you see, the room looked it."

"You were wrong," he said quietly. "'The fact is, that I get ten thousand a year from the estate of my dead aunt. I tell you this, not because I am at all purse proud, but because I do not think you would readily room with a pauper."

I was silent for a moment, but when I answered I had fully made up my mind.

"After seeing your work," I cried, "I would room with you if you hadn't a cent. A wise man hitches his wagon to a star, and tries to reflect a little of its brilliancy. The thing is settled so far as I am concerned."

We shook hands on it, there and then, and Paul and I started for home as the clock struck midnight.

"Don't you agree with me now, that he will be a great man some day?" cried Paul an hour later as he jumped into bed?

"No," I replied with warmth, "not some day. He is already a great man!"

III

The careless ways
Of college days
Are gone, old man, are gone.

The spring term of my last year in college sped with winged feet. Little or nothing I saw of Martin, for I was working day and night for the final examinations, and had time for nothing else. I heard of him frequently from my brother, however, who had become his admiring familiar spirit. The boy bettered himself by this friendship, and no longer thought, as he formerly did, that it was manly to come home a little the worse for liquor. All this pleased me, and I did everything to strengthen the relations between them, little thinking what the future would bring forth.

I succeeded in squeezing through the examinations, more by luck than good judgment, and went home to my people the proud possessor of a B.A. from the University.

The summer months passed by, and I heard from Martin frequently through letters addressed to Paul.

At last the day of our departure for Paris arrived, and my brother accompanied me to the ship to say a last good-by. Martin was already there, his thin face bronzed by a summer spent at the seashore. I can see him yet as he shook Paul's hand. The deep solemnity of his expression and the great soft light in his eyes were completely foreign to the man.

"Good-by, Paul," he said. "And leave the drink alone," he added, "for it is the worst enemy you can ever have."

My brother was strangely moved by his words, and I saw the tears glisten in his eyes.

"I'll try," he said simply, and he was gone in the crowd.

The voyage over was an uneventful one, and it is a waste of time to describe it here. Suffice it to say we arrived in Paris safely, and secured a suite of three rooms in the Latin Quarter, an unusual extravagance there. Martin's sleeping apartment, the one in which he spent most of his time, he kept, true to his ideals, as bare and uncomfortable as possible. I did not share these peculiar views of his and in consequence the other two rooms were fitted up in all the elegance that the long purse of a loving father could command. My roommate contributed his half of this in spite of my protests, saying it was but fair that we should share in all things. Indeed, I ever found him free to the point of lavishness with his money.

Those were happy days for me. I enjoyed the free life of the Latin Quarter to the uttermost, and loved my art passionately, with all the ardor of a boy. I did well with my work, and received the congratulations of my fellow students accordingly. Once even the great Julien had stopped before a drawing of mine longer than was his wont.

"Ah, monsieur, you have some talent, and your heart is in it. All this I can see at a glance," he had said, and then he passed on to Martin, who sat next me. The model on that day I remember to have been a French peasant in rough homespun.

I turned instinctively to hear his comment on my roommate's work. Julien was standing, with a perplexed frown on his face, gazing at Martin's canvas fixedly.

"It is good—very good," I heard him mutter, "and yet there is something lacking. Ah, I have it!" he cried a moment later. "Your heart is not in it like your young compatriot's here," and he tapped me on the shoulder. "You like not this kind of work. Am I not right, Monsieur Martin?"

"Perfectly," replied Martin with a grim smile. "The model is not to my taste."

I knew of Julien's hasty temper, and was prepared for a burst of anger at this, but it never came.

"Quite so," he said mildly. "Every artist has his likes and dislikes. Let us say then that you choose a model for yourself," he continued, "and bring me the painting when it is finished. Is a month enough time?"

"Plenty," said Martin, and the great man passed on.

Six weeks had gone by since our arrival in Paris, by which time I had made a host of young artists my friends. They would drop into the rooms at all hours for a glass of rare wine or a choice cigar (luxuries with which I was well supplied, thanks to my father's generosity), and in a little while my college French was improved a hundred per cent.

Martin, however, liked seclusion, and especially after that conversation with Julien. Often I would not see him for days together, and when I did it was only for a few minutes at a time. He would leave early in the morning, with his portfolio under his arm, and then would not return again till night. Even the few hours that he was home he would spend locked up in his own room, no matter how many students were visiting me at the time. At last, on this account, he became known to all as the mysterious Martin. To tell the truth, I was rather relieved than otherwise by his aloofness, for the man got on my nerves. When he was about I always felt a strange irritation, for which I was at a loss to account. Now, as I look back at it, I think it was that ever-present atmosphere of power that he had about him that was as gall and wormwood to my own no small conceit.

I remember one night, while the champagne corks were popping merrily, and song and laughter filled the air, Martin's door suddenly opened and he stepped into our midst, his face a deathly white and great black hollows under his eyes. The noise died away on the instant.

"Welcome, stranger!" cried I in forced heartiness. "Have you come to join the merrymakers?"

"Just so," said he, and he poured himself a glass of wine, and drank it down at a gulp.

"What have you been doing with yourself?" asked one of the others. "You're as pale as a ghost."

"Living with a corpse for a month," said Martin slowly. "Would you like to see it?"

A deathlike silence greeted his strange words. What could he mean, I wondered? Was the man mad?

"Well, no one seems over-anxious," he continued; "but I'll get it just the same," and he turned on his heel and entered his room once more.

For one terrible moment I had a mental picture of his dragging in a dead body by the hair, and I was bathed in a cold sweat from head to foot, then I was plunged into a fit of well-nigh hysterical laughter, as were those about me, for he returned with only a painting under his arm.

"Sorry to disappoint you," he said listlessly, "but I think this will inspire something of the same feelings that the model would cause," and he placed the canvas on the mantelpiece, where we could all see it.

Again there was a perfect silence, broken only by the hard breathing of those about me. All eyes were glued upon the painting. Then slowly, one by one, we arose, and silently, with awe written deep on each man's face, we shook Martin's hand. It was the highest tribute I have ever seen paid to a living artist, in its absolute sincerity. There were two or three men present that night, who were afterward to become international figures in art, but at that moment we knew in our souls that there was but one great master living, and his name was Martin.

You will ask, what was in this picture to move us so? It is beyond my feeble pen to describe the sensations of horror with which it filled me. Horror, I might say, to well-nigh the point of nausea, was mine, and yet even that falls short of the mark.

The painting represented the morgue in the dim, unearthly twilight, and more especially one figure in the place. This was the body of a man, evidently found drowned, for it was swollen to unnatural size, lying on the usual marble slab. The skin of the dead face was a horrible mottled green shade, and the protruding eyes were covered with a kind of fungus, while to add to its horror, the unshaved chin had dropped, disclosing two yellow fangs in a ghastly grin. On either side of this grim figure, stretching away in the semi-gloom, were other slabs, each with its occupant, and each the bed of some new fantastic terror. Underneath the whole thing was written in English the four words, He Laughs at Death.

We drank to Martin with brimming glasses, we sang and laughed, while he for the nonce laid aside his cloak of aloofness, and was the wildest there. He told us stories so grotesquely droll that we roared with laughter, until our glances unconsciously reverted to the painting, then I thought I saw his eyes glitter in triumph, as the laughter died away, and the smiles disappeared from our faces as though by magic.

He was a strange man.

IV

High above the stars are shining,
    Whispering to one another,
All set in the silver lining
    Of the sky, brother to brother.

On the next day Martin showed Julien his painting.
Never will I forget the expression on the little Frenchman's
face as he stood before my roommate's easel. Admiration
and awe were mirrored there for the world to see.

"And you did this?" he said at last. "Do you know
what this work is, my friend?"

"I think it is pretty good," said Martin coolly.

"Good?" cried Julien in a tone that made every student
in the room look up. "Good?" he continued excitedly. "Why,
it stands alone in art. It is the masterpiece of the terrible,
and you call it only pretty good. There the cold-blooded
American speaks. Yes," he went on, in an admirable imitation
of Martin's slow drawl, "let me assure you, monsieur, it is,

as you say, pretty good, and also, M. Martin, it is the work of a master of masters, before whom Julien feels very small, and what you call afraid." So saying, the emotional little man, trembling all over as from an attack of the ague, left the room.

Pandemonium broke loose on the instant. No sooner had the door closed behind him than Martin was surrounded by art students. Cries of admiration, wonder and worship arose on all sides, until one could not hear oneself speak. I could see by the expression on my roommate's face that he hated this sort of thing, and it was not long before he made his escape through the door, his picture held tight under his arm.

In very truth I had hitched my wagon to a star, and the reflected glory of that star was mine. I was besieged constantly in my rooms by a host of friends. I was dined and wined by a multitude, who wished to meet the eccentric master artist, Martin. He, however, would have nothing to do with any of them, and pretended sickness so as not to meet them, until the first fine edge of the excitement wore off. In a few days they had given him up as hopeless, and things had fallen back in the old channels again.

Time passed, and before we knew it, a year had rolled by. Martin had worked consistently, and now the walls of our studio were covered with horrors. You can have no idea of the weird feeling one had in that room when the lights burnt low. It was as though you were sitting in a charnal house, and the very air seemed cold and damp, like that in a tomb.

One night this feeling was stronger upon me than ever before. I hadn't felt well all day, and as I sat before the dying fire alone the flickering light would reveal first one stiffening horror and then another, till my taxed nerves could stand no more.

Finally I jumped up, and with a muttered curse, turned each one of the grisly pictures to the wall. Just as I had finished I heard a low laugh behind me, and wheeled around to face Martin, who had entered as noiselessly as a cat. His sallow face still wore a crooked, evil smile, while the tip of his tongue moistened his upper lip.

"So it is just as Julien said to-day," he cried. "No one will buy my pictures because they are too realistic in their horror, and if they are sold by any chance they will be soon banished to the attic, for who would live with the dead except Martin, and he doesn't understand those cold ones, even he," and again the red tip of his tongue moistened his upper lip.

It may have been the fervor creeping over me, but at his words I felt a deadly nausea at the pit of my stomach, and the strange sensation of having some precious secret drawn from me against my will, the same feeling, in fact, as I had experienced once before, only now much more intense. Then followed a dizzy helplessness, and all things spun round and round, and faded into blackness.

I had fainted.

V

Sailing, sailing thru storms that rise in the night
Sailing, sailing, in sickness, fever and fright,
    With bellying sail
    That catches the gale,
And our star for a beacon light.

For the duration of a whole week I was delirious with
typhoid fever. Strange dreams were mine, and in these
Martin was ever the centre figure. One I still remember, and
as it made such a lasting impression on me I will tell it here.

I felt that I was lying on a bed of coals in the
bottomless abyss of hell. Surrounding me on all sides were
devil shapes, that watched my sufferings gleefully. Repeatedly
I tried to rise from my scorching couch, but at each of my
attempts I was pushed violently back again. Just as my
sufferings were at their height, Martin's lean face would bend
over me, while his gray eyes would gaze into mine with a

curious look, and his cold voice would say, "How do you feel now."

At those moments the old sensation of nausea would return, followed by the black mists of unconsciousness to put an end to my torments for the time being. This strange dream was repeated a score of times, and thus my vivid recollection of it.

As I have said, it was a full week before I regained my reason. I was lying on my own bed when I opened my eyes, and the sun was streaming in through a window above my head. I lay there gazing at the broad band of light it made upon my pillow with all the curiosity of a new-born child. Suddenly it occurred to me, that I would like to touch its warming ray, so I attempted to lift one of my wasted hands, resting on the coverlet beside me. What was my surprise to find that, try as I would, this simple thing was beyond me, and that it took all of my strength to slide it along, let alone lift it from the bed.

"How do you feel now?" came Martin's voice from beside me.

I had not seen him, and the sudden start of surprise, coupled with his words, which were exactly as he had used in my dream, brought back the old giddiness, and I fainted once more.

When I again regained consciousness I felt much better, and was even strong enough to move my head from side to side. I saw Martin and a gray-haired man, who proved to be Dr. Copiens, talking earnestly at the door. Finally the old man left, and my roommate tip-toed back to the bed. As he sat down in a chair beside me, he noticed that my eyes were open, and he immediately put his finger on his lip to command my silence. Soon I fell gently to sleep.

Each day I grew stronger, and gradually my temperature descended to normal. Martin was my only nurse. Sitting beside me all day long, he helped to while away the tedious hours with his wonderful knack of story telling. Listening to him, I forgot the pangs of hunger that assailed me, for under Dr. Copiens' care, milk was my only food, and I sometimes dreamed of juicy beefsteaks and other good things, till I fairly gnashed my teeth in weak impotency.

As I have said, Martin caused me to forget my troubles with his tales. It was not the stories themselves that held me, for he would often repeat those that I had already heard, but his wonderful wording, that made them run as smoothly as a river of oil, and was as pleasant to the ear as music.

Sometimes I would speak of my brother, and then always Martin was the eager listener. I had received several letters from home, and one in particular from my father that had worried me. In it he more than hinted that Paul was drinking again.

"I can do nothing with him," it ran. "After a drinking bout he is plunged into such a state of mind that the slightest reprimand, I feel convinced, would drive him to any lengths, even to the taking of his own life. I wish you were home. Perhaps you could help him."

This came while I was still very weak, and so Martin read it to me aloud. His face darkened as he perused the lines I quote here, and he bit his lip in anger.

"It's in his blood," I heard him mutter. "I could handle him, but another would take the wrong way, and that would be fatal."

"You must think a whole lot of the boy?" I ventured.

"A whole lot?" he burst forth with flaming eyes. "And why do you think I wasted all these days pulling you out of the valley of death if I didn't? You blind little imitation artist you might even now be roasting in hell if you hadn't been his brother," and he jumped to his feet and left the room.

I was surprised into silence, yet strangely relieved at his words. I never had liked the man, and to be weighed down under a load of obligations to one we dislike is a very unpleasant experience. If he had not done these things for me, but for another, surely I owed him nothing, I reasoned, and the thought pleased me mightily. How easily we can throw dust in our own eyes.

In a few days more I was sitting up in a chair, propped with cushions. My temperature had been normal now for a long time, nearly two weeks, and I was allowed to eat about what I pleased once more. Oh, the incredible delight of eating, to a man just recovered from typhoid. It fairly makes up for all the earlier sufferings, and fulfills a host of famished dreams.

As I have said, I was sitting up in a chair, and thinking contentedly of the dinner that was soon to be served. Already the pleasant odor of it, wafting in through the half-opened door, caused my nostrils to dilate in anticipation. Shortly our landlady's heavy tread would sound on the stairway, and then she would appear with the steaming tray in her hands, and I licked my lips at the thought. Just at this moment Martin's door opened, and he entered, dragging his trunk after him with both hands. A mutual coldness had sprung up between us since his strange speech about my brother, but this unusual sight caused me to forget it for the moment.

"Where are you going?" I cried in astonishment.

"Home," he answered, without glancing up.

"Not to America?" I asked.

"Where else?" said he, and he began to tighten the trunk straps.

"But your art?" I cried. "How about your painting?"

"Oh," he answered in a matter-of-fact tone, "I'm going to give that up."

"Give it up?" I fairly shouted. "After what Julien has said? You would be recognized by the whole world in a year or so as a great master, and now you talk of giving it up. Why, man, you're stark mad."

"Do you think so?" he said coldly, still bending over the trunk.

"I know so," I answered with heat. "What else could you turn your hand to with the same success? Art, such as yours, springs from the soul. You would be tearing out the best part of you."

"You are right," he cried. "I will have to do that in the career that I am planning for myself."

"What is this precious career?" I asked sneeringly.

"Literature," he answered, looking up for the first time. "I took up art merely to illustrate my own stories. No other man could do them justice."

"So you are one of that numerous band of young men who think they can write?" I cried with a laugh that brought the blood to his sallow cheeks. "What reason have you to suppose so? You never even took up literature in college."

"But you must admit that I can tell a story," he said simply.

"Yes," I replied grudgingly, for his absolute confidence in his own ability grated on me. "But they are not original," I hastened to add, "while to create you must have imagination, which, you tell me yourself, you lack entirely. Then again," I continued, "you do not mingle enough with other men, and therefore you are ignorant of human nature. A man to become a great writer, I was quoting Dr. Johnstone, must be a student and admirer of his fellow man, or else he misses the human touch. You must agree with me there," I finished.

"On the contrary," said Martin in a tone that he might have used to a tiresome child, "you are wrong, entirely wrong."

"How so?" I demanded hotly.

"Well, in the first place," he continued, "because a man doesn't need imagination. I, myself, have what is far better, a concise memory, and the ability to put down on paper, in the best wording, exactly what I see or feel. There is enough going on in this old world at the present moment to make a million stories, and a man has but to get off the beaten track to find it. So much for your first reason. Then you say that I am a recluse, in which you are right, and that I miss the human touch on that account, in which you are wrong. It seems to me that an onlooker, a mere spectator, with no party feeling of any kind, sees more of a battle than the actual participants, and the same is true of the battle of life. Finally you say that a writer should love and admire his fellow man. Why, if we love and admire a thing, we can see but the one side of that thing, the good side, and therefore, in the case of our fellow man, we miss the larger half of faults and follies that go to make up the human race. No," he finished with a faint sneer, "I think you have missed the mark altogether."

"Maybe you are right," I growled; "but at any rate, you're a fool to throw away a certainty for an obscure possibility. Besides, have you stopped to think that the author of to-day has to cater to the mob, as you call them?"

"But with my style of work it won't be necessary," he cried with flashing eyes. "An accident happens on the street. In a moment hundreds have collected, drawn by the curious love for the terrible, a human trait. In my stories, that same throbbing sensation of horror will be ever present. People will buy them by the thousands, and going home to comforts and safety, experience the delightful feeling of tragedy by their own firesides. Who would not go around the corner to see a murder? All would go, if they could do it with safety to themselves, and therefore they will snatch up my work, that will give them the exact sensations of seeing the crime being committed."

His eyes were glowing strangely as he spoke, and I found myself growing enthusiastic at his words, in spite of my doubts.

"But," I cried, "do you think that you can create that feeling in the minds of your readers? If you can, you will be a great writer, but if you can't, what then?"

"There is no such word as failure in my vocabulary," said Martin coldly. "I will surely succeed as a writer, as surely, indeed, as you will fail as an artist."

"What do you mean?" I shouted angrily. "Julien thinks highly of my work. He told me so."

"Yes," he replied, "it is good now, for you paint things as they are, but later, when you are out in the world, it will be different."

"In what way?" I asked, slightly mollified.

"Because," he continued, "the successful portrait painter—I am speaking from the worldly commercial standpoint when I use the word successful—must be nothing more nor less than a beauty doctor. In other words, people do not wish to be painted as they look in reality, but as they would wish to look, or it may be as they imagine they do look. Bring out a good feature, help a bad one, and yet keep a slight resemblance there of your wealthy patron, so that the poor relations will at least know who it is supposed to be and can enthuse accordingly, and then you become what the world considers a successful artist. What a soul-inspiring vocation. Remember your watchword through life shall be, 'When I touch a man's vanity I also touch his money bags,'" and he laughed as he left the room.

"I will never do that, not if I have to starve first!" I cried after him as he went down the stairs, but a taunting laugh was my only answer.

VI

The cold wind came from the world about
And then sighing blew the lights all out.
    The reflecting stone
    No longer shone
The face the poor fool thought his own.

Martin sailed that same week, and, to tell the truth, I was very glad to be rid of him. He left all of his paintings behind, and no sooner had I seen him safe on his ship than I tore his grewsome work from the wall, and replaced it with brighter things. Julien learned of this in some way, and he offered, what I considered at the time, a very high price for them, which I immediately accepted. Now, I understand, they are considered practically priceless, and are exhibited beside the old masters, but then I was happy in my ignorance, jingling the gold pieces in my pocket, so what did it matter?

I soon found another roommate, and the months went by merrily. Every now and then I would get a letter from home telling me all the news. My brother, it seemed, had at last reformed, and the thing had come about through a friend by the name of Martin. "He has such a good influence over Paul," wrote my mother, "and yet somehow I cannot bring myself to like him. I think it is his peculiar air of power that affects me disagreeably," she went on. "I always feel nervous, and yet extremely cautious in his company, as though I had a secret that I must keep from him at all costs. This is nonsense, of course, but it is exactly as I feel." The rest of the letter was on an entirely different subject, and I will omit it here.

Time passed away, and finally two years had elapsed since Martin had left the studio. One fine spring morning the blow fell. I saw a letter lying on my dresser, and recognizing Paul's writing, I opened it with a smile on my lips.

The very first words that I read caused the smile to leave my lips, and the letter to flutter down at my feet. It told me of my father's death from a stroke of apoplexy, and of his total failure in the business world. At first, of course, his death meant everything and the money part of it never entered my head, but on the long trip home, it is to be confessed, the vision of a well-appointed studio in New York rose before my eyes many times, the dearer to me now because it was beyond my means.

I found things at home even worse than I had expected. My father had not only died a bankrupt, but had toward the last incurred heavy debts, no doubt to keep me in Paris, thinking that something would turn up to put him on his feet again. The one pleasant surprise was my brother.

The town of Merlin, where my family lived, had
voted a year before to prohibit the sale of liquor principally
through the united efforts of Martin and Paul. They had
worked day and night canvassing votes, and finally had won
by a close majority.

"And I haven't had a drink since," said Paul. "Somehow,
when the stuff is not to be bought on every corner, it doesn't
bother me any. I graduate this summer from Law School,"
he continued proudly, "and when I start in practice I ought
to rake in the money with both hands, at least so Martin
says."

"Do you see much of him now?" I asked.

"No," he answered rather regretfully. "You see, he lives
over on the East Side in New York, gathering material for a
book that he's writing. He says that he can get me enough
criminal cases to make my fortune. He's hand-and-glove
with them, and has to be to draw them out. Every now and
then he drops out here, though, and tells me some story
that keeps me awake all night with its horror. He has great
genius that way."

"Has he had anything in the magazines yet?" I asked.

"Yes, one story in *Everybodies' Friend*. Here it is," and
he handed me a magazine. "Read it," he continued, "while I
go down town," and he swung open the gate and left me.

I opened the *Everybodies' Friend*, and on the very first
page my eyes encountered a drawing of Martin's. It was a
miniature of the first painting I had ever seen of his, the
girl lying dead in the snow, only now it had been touched
up till it fairly stood out of the background of dull gray, a
masterpiece. Even in the daylight I felt a cold shiver creep
up my back, and my gaze was held by it, as steel is held
by the magnet. At last, with an effort, I turned to the next

page. The Murder of Mary Mortimer was the title of the story, and underneath it was Martin's full name.

"Something trashy, I suppose," I said to myself, and then started to read.

From the first page I knew that I was wrong, entirely wrong, although I tried to blind myself to it. If the man's drawing was horrible and yet great, his story was diabolic and yet a classic. I felt the same feelings arise in me that the deformed half-idiot hero felt in the story, when the voice whispered in his ear, "You are losing her, and it's better to have her dead."

Then, when he is driven by the voice to strike her down a red ruin in the snow, the whole scene seemed to dance before my eyes, and my hands grasped the arms of the chair in weak impotency, while all unconsciously I cried aloud, "Stop it, stop it!"

"I see you like my story," said a voice beside me.

I looked up and encountered the cold gray eyes of the author, Martin. Involuntarily my hand went up to my forehead, and then came down again, dripping wet. I was perspiring at every pore, as though I had run a race. I gathered myself together with a mighty effort, and rose to my feet to grasp his hand.

"Wonderful!" I cried in a shaking voice, "wonderful! The most realistic thing I ever read," I continued after a moment's pause. "Surely you must have imagination to write like that?"

"No," he replied with a smile, "I got the theme of the story second-handed. I meet some strange characters. But where is Paul? Downtown? Well, I think I'll look him up," and he was off.

He left me still under the influence of the story, and when his tall figure had vanished down the street I arose, and still trembling, entered the house, where I placed the magazine gently in the glowing grate, and then I took a long breath of relief.

This occurred on the second day of my home-coming, and a week later found me painting my first portrait. Our straitened circumstances compelled immediate money getting, and so I had written to many of my old college friends, asking if they knew of anything in my line, and not hiding the fact that I was in a pretty tight place financially. By return mail I received an answer to one of these. It was from a wealthy young fellow named Browne, who said, in his jollying way, that his mother was dying to have her face immortalized by my brush. Could I come the next day?

I surely could, and did, to find Mrs. Browne awaiting me impatiently. She was one of those nervous scrawny women who consider themselves young and beautiful at fifty, and are a bugbear to all artists. She would never sit still a minute, and a continual stream of small-talk gurgled from her lips.

"When would it be done? Was it true that the artist could not only depict the face and form, but also the inner being, the soul, yes, that was it, the soul on the canvas?" etc.

I felt like asking her what her soul looked like, but luckily I refrained.

"No, I won't look at it now, not until it is finished. It will be such a surprise then," she tittered.

I knew what was coming, but I went on grimly, and painted her exactly as she was. At last it was finished, and she gazed at it for one fell moment, then gasped with horror, regained her dignity with a mighty effort, and swept out of the room, with all the self-consciousness of a hen that has trod in a puddle.

I was left alone to my gloomy reflections. I had failed to please with my first portrait, and yet I knew it contained the best work of which I was capable. Was Martin right, after all, in saying that an artist to succeed must be a beauty doctor? Evidently so, or at least my first experience indicated as much. Then I needed the money badly, and yet had been so sure of myself that I had told Mrs. Browne to pay me whatever she thought the painting to be worth, as I had no fixed price. What a fool I had been. I could tell now what she thought it was worth by the expression on her face, and the bills at home piled up on my desk, danced before my eyes.

"What's the trouble?" I heard a voice say.

I looked up in surprise to see George Browne standing beside me.

"Nothing," I answered a trifle unsteadily. "The picture," and I pointed to it with a trembling finger, "doesn't please your mother, that's all."

"You don't say so," said he a little vaguely, and he stepped forward and gazed at the portrait fixedly.

For a moment only he stood thus, and then he burst into a laugh that echoed through the silent room. This was the crowning insult. I felt the blood throbbing in my temples, and my hands were clenching convulsively in anger.

"So you think it poor, even ridiculous?" I cried through white lips.

He turned around on his heel, his face still red from laughter.

"Not at all," he chuckled, "for it's the best thing I ever saw. Looks exactly like her, and that's the funny part of it."

"How so?" I asked, bewildered.

"Why, just look, man," he cried, putting one hand on my shoulder, while he pointed with the other, "you've even got the wrinkles on her face and neck, and the crows' feet under her eyes. She looks every inch herself, and a good fifty years old, there's where the humor comes in. She expected you to make her look like sweet sixteen, and you haven't even given her the benefit of the doubt—powder and rouge. No wonder she's sore, and what's more, she thinks she has a right to be. But fix it up, old man, and she'll come around all right."

"Fix it up?" I repeated dully after him. "Fix it up? Why, it couldn't be a better likeness of her if I worked a year on it."

"But haven't I told you," he broke in impatiently, "that she don't want it to look like her. She wants it to look like what she thinks she looks like. Besides, what do you care so long as you sell the picture. The money is what you want."

"Don't you think, Browne," I said, "that there's such a thing as loving art for art's sake, I mean, beside the money part of it?"

"There might have been a hundred years ago," he answered; "but now we live in an age of money, and the artist has to be a business man also, or, in other words, supply the people with goods they want. If he fails to do this, he starves or gets a new job, so fall in line, Charley, fall in line, and touch up the mater's picture as a good beginning."

For a long time after he had left me, I stood staring out of the window, seeing nothing but the piled up bills that lay on my desk at home, and the white face of my mother. At last, with a feeling of regret, I picked up my discarded brush once more and started beautifying the likeness of Mrs. Browne. Somehow I felt that I was a beaten man, who had finally fallen in line, and there was a bitterness and self-loathing imbedded in my very soul.

"I would rather eat bread and cheese the rest of my life, and do the work that is in me, than take all that the world has to offer and be a living lie," Martin had said, but he was a man apart from other men.

VII

Fair romance, beauty, art and life,
  They seek thus to fire again;
But what they find is sordid strife,
  The whole world a trader's den.

I had failed as an artist, but had succeeded as a
business man. Mrs. Browne fell into ecstacies over her
portrait, and gave me a large check accordingly.

"Just fancy," she said, "I thought it was finished that
first time I looked at it; but it wasn't, was it?"

"No, of course not," I hastened to reply.

"How stupid of me," she cried. "Really at first, you
know, I was very disappointed, but now that it is completed,
I'm delighted with it, and will show it to all my friends, not
forgetting to mention the name of the artist as well," and
she beamed upon me.

I felt the blood burning in my cheeks as I stammered
out some words of thanks, and then I hurriedly left the

house, fearing that my tongue would betray my real feelings, that were so entirely the reverse of what she imagined. Somehow, when the door shut behind me, I realized that I was leaving a poorer man than I had come. It was true that I had a check in my pocket to keep away the wolf from the door, but in its place I had left the best part of me—my art.

Time passed, and I became, what the world would call, a very successful portrait painter. Mrs. Browne had been as good as her word, and had recommended me to a score of wealthy friends. Some of them gave me a trial, and I beautified them to their hearts' content, with the result that I became universally in demand.

Soon I was able to fit out a studio in New York, and thus fulfilled one of my youthful dreams. My mother was destined never to see the world at my feet, for, shortly after my home-coming, she caught a cold that gradually settled into pneumonia. She had been broken down in health ever since the death of my father, and so the end came quickly. Now, as I look back on it, I heartily thank God that He took her when he did, for thus she missed the great load of suffering that would have been in store for her had she lived.

But now, that I had everything that money could buy, I was not a happy man. My work became drudgery that palled upon me, and I felt discontented and irritable, as though my nerves were continually on edge. I had to drive myself to my tasks, and the spur that kept me going, the only flash of sunlight in my black horizon, was the knowledge that in a few years I could save enough to retire, and lead a life of leisure. Meanwhile I received the praise of the mass mind, and writhed under it, knowing it to be only the dollar sign that they paid homage to, and for which I had sold myself.

At those times the words of Martin echoed in my brain: "From superior men we sink to the position of the organ-grinder's monkey that is pelted with pennies. He amuses the crowd with his grotesque antics, and so do we. It may be that the world does not know this, but we know it, and that's what hurts." Yes, I was in that position, and it galled me to the soul.

Paul passed his examinations to the bar, and soon was making money hand over fist, as he had predicted. No sooner had he hung out his shingle than a crowd of clients besieged him at all hours. They were evil-looking men for the most part, dressed in rags and tatters, yet, for all that, they paid his fees without a whimper. He was soon able to buy a pretentious house on Riverside Drive, for he had taken Martin's advice, and had moved to New York shortly after mother's death. He would often exasperate me by giving my old roommate credit for his success.

"Yes," he would say, glancing about his well-appointed library, "I owe all this to him. He cured me of drunkenness and sent me my clients."

"Maybe so," I would interrupt; "but if you didn't know enough law to win the majority of your cases, and if you weren't strong enough to leave the drink alone, I don't think that he could do you much good."

But he would only shake his head at this and repeat over again, like a child learning a lesson:

"I owe everything to him—everything."

Then I would get red with anger, for I could never forgive Martin his prophecy. He had told me that I would become what I now was, and I hated him for it.

"How about his book?" I would cry. "If he can make other people, he don't seem to be able to make himself. For over two years he's been working on the thing, and yet there don't seem to be any results. Won't the publishers take it?"

"How do I know?" Paul would say. "He never talks about his work. But I'll tell you this," he would continue, his face flushing and his eyes sparkling, "when he does finish it, you'll know it, and what's more, the whole world will know it."

One night we were arguing as usual about the man. I had just made an allusion to his book in practically the same words that are quoted above, but this time Paul answered nothing, and rising to his feet he crossed the room to a table that stood in a corner, and then returned with something in his hand.

"What do you call this?" said he, and he tossed a book into my lap. "Many Murders" was the title on the cover, and underneath it was Martin's name. I felt crestfallen and foolish.

"So he has finished it at last?" I growled.

"Yes," cried Paul enthusiastically, "and the thing will be a classic."

"Don't be so sure of that," I replied with a sneer. "To my mind it is more likely to be highly sensational than great."

"Then you are wrong," Paul said, and he picked up a paper beside him, and read the following lines: "'I think that Martin's "Many Murders" contains the greatest piece of horror writing since the days of Poe, and in my opinion indeed even that gifted genius had not the realistic touch that makes "Many Murders" a masterpiece of the terrible,'" etc., etc. Signed to this article was the name of the greatest living critic, Sir Vivian Gerard.

"What do you say to that?" asked Paul.

"Nothing at all," I answered, "for when Gerard says a thing, it is not for me to contradict. Have you read it yet?"

"Yes," said he; "and I couldn't go to sleep all last night on account of it. Take it home with you if you want to."

I acted on his suggestion, and an hour later found me home, with the book open on my knee. It is a needless waste of time to describe here my feelings as I perused it. You, my readers, have felt the same strange mixture of fascination and fear, as you have bent over the illustrations. You, my readers, have thrilled in excitement to freeze to horror, as you read of those terrible murders, that are described so vividly, that it is as though you saw them with your own eyes.

Suffice it to say that I, like my brother, slept very little that night.

VIII

Bring in the dead
    And crown that listless brow.
Its thoughts have fled.
    A vacant temple now
      Of spirits gone.
Bring in the dead.

The sensation caused by Martin's book soon took to itself gigantic proportions. It set the whole literary world agog for many months. Critical praise and censure appeared in all the leading magazines, and many pens of international fame were wielded in its justification or its condemnation. It is to be noted that none of these called it an average book. No, it was classified as either a very great work, or else the sensational nightmare of a disordered brain. Meanwhile the public became excited, and bought it by the thousands. Sir Vivian Gerard wrote an article for one of the periodicals, in which he said, as far as his experience went, it was the first great classic to become a best seller immediately after its appearance. Gradually the majority of the critics came around to his way of thinking, and, in spite of professional jealousy in some cases, grudgingly conceded it a place at the summit of American literature.

Years went by, and I saw very little of Martin. Sometimes I met him at Paul's house, where, in spite of the fact that he was now one of the shining lights of the world, he was a frequent visitor. I avoided him as much as I could for two reasons: One was that I felt that he was laughing inwardly to see his prophecy concerning my art prove to be correct, while the other was the feeling of inferiority I always experienced in his presence that was so sorely antagonistic to my own no small ego.

About three years after his book had won him fame, he came into my studio accompanied by Paul. I was engaged at the time retouching a portrait of a Mrs. Vandeveer, who was a prominent figure in the society world, and was so intent upon my work that I hadn't noticed their presence till Martin spoke.

"And who is that supposed to be?" came his cold voice from behind my chair.

I started like a guilty schoolboy. "Mrs. Vandeveer," I faltered. "But it isn't finished yet," I hastened to explain.

"Just so," said he. "I've known her for quite a while. My eyes must be failing me."

"No, it's not that," I cried bitterly, throwing discretion to the winds. "I know it looks no more like her than her own daughter does, but a man must live."

"Yes," he said, "that's what Padlock Jones told me the day before he murdered the Jew. It's a good old saying, and many a brave man has adorned the end of a rope because of it."

Paul hastened to break in at that, seeing the hot anger written on my face, no doubt.

"Cut out your shop talk," he cried, "and listen to me, Charley. Mart and I are going up to the Maine woods for a little vacation, and we thought that you might join us. What's the good word?"

I noticed Martin's face brighten, as I replied that it was impossible, and I cursed the man properly in my heart for it.

"Awfully sorry, old man," said Paul as he shook my hand in leave-taking. "We'll be back in a couple of months, and will see you then. Be good."

"Yes," echoed Martin, "be good and stick to business," after which parting shot the door slammed behind them and they were gone.

I looked out of the window, and saw them walking down the street, arm in arm. The strange contrast between the two men struck me more forcibly at that moment than ever before. Paul, so big and full of life, while beside him glided, with a catlike tread, the slim ascetic figure of Martin.

"Like an evil shadow," I said to myself, as I returned to my work once more. "Two months is a long time," I muttered a little later. "Paul will be back before then; he'll grow tired of it."

I was right. He came home before the two months had passed, but it was not as I expected.

Three weeks later to the day, a knock sounded on my studio door.

"Come in," I shouted, and a messenger boy entered.

"A telegram for you, sir," said he, with his hat in his hand.

Who could be sending me a wire, I wondered, as I signed the book he held out to me. My brother it must be, I concluded as the boy went off whistling. He's probably killed some big game, a moose possibly, and he wants to tell me of it. That's like him, sure enough.

In spite of my reasoning, I tore open the yellow envelope with trembling fingers. "Paul is dead. Am bringing him home by the four-fifteen," were the words that fairly burnt themselves into my brain.

"Paul is dead," I repeated slowly as in a dream, and before my eyes appeared the old room at New Haven, and the bright face framed in the doorway, smiling at me.

"I'm home again, Charley," it seemed to say.

"No," I answered dully, "never again. Paul is dead."

Thus it was that the true horror of it descended upon me for the first time, and the room swam round and round. Then, as had happened so many years ago in Paris, the black veil of unconsciousness descended upon me, blotting out every thing.

IX

Tell them of the waving grasses,
    Nodding gayly over head,
And of the soft step that passes
    Lightly o'er their earthy bed.

When I again regained consciousness, the studio was in the semi-gloom of twilight. All remembrance, of the blow that had fallen on me, was for the time completely banished from my mind. I was like a man waking from a sleep of nightmares, trembling in every limb, and yet unable to account for my condition. Why was I lying on the floor, and what was that I held in my hand, were the thoughts that puzzled me.

Slowly I opened my tightly clenched fist, and saw the crumpled ball of yellow paper that lay in my palm. "A telegram," I said to myself, and then like a flash my memory returned.

"But it can't be true," I cried aloud; "it can't be true," and I staggered to my feet, and reeled to the window like a drunken man.

Already the sky was crimson from the setting sun, that peered at me over the endless stretch of housetops, and the paper in my hand reddened in its last rays, as though it had been dipped in blood, yet through it the words stood out in frightful distinctness, as though they had grown larger in the lurid light.

"Paul is dead. Am bringing him home on the four-fifteen," I repeated dully, and instinctively I pulled out my watch and looked at it. "Six o'clock," I muttered, "and too late," and then again, "Paul is dead."

I felt no pain at the time, only a kind of stupid wonderment, that Paul, so strong and so full of animal spirits, should be dead. It seemed monstrous and inconceivable. At that moment I could have believed that the world would end, but that Paul should die, that seemed the impossible and absurd thing.

There must be some mistake, I reasoned. Surely there are other Pauls and other Martins as well. It was all a mistake, a surprising coincidence, nothing more. The boy had given me a telegram addressed to some one else, some one who had had a loved one named Paul that had died, an invalid, most probably, long ailing, and not at all like my big, healthy brother, who had never had a sickness in his life. Yes, that was surely it, and I started searching the darkening room for the envelope.

Finally I picked it up, where it had fallen on the floor, and went back to the window, and then a groan burst from my throat, for my full name, Charles P. Smithers, was written on it in a clear hand.

Just at this moment I heard stumbling footsteps on the stairs outside, as though some one was coming up with a heavy load. A terrible thought crossed my throbbing brain. They were bringing my dead brother up to me, that was it. They were carrying him stiff and stark up the stairs that groaned under their weight. They would lay him on the couch there, where the red light would stream upon him through the window. Instinctively I pulled down the shades, and touched the electric button that illumined the room.

At that moment the door opened, and Martin strode in. Even in my mental condition I noticed the altered appearance of the man. He seemed to have grown ten years older in those short three weeks, and his face was heavily lined and as gray as a death's head. The rims of his shifting eyes were red as from prolonged weeping, but his voice, when he spoke, was metallic in its utter lack of feeling.

"How is this?" he said. "Didn't you get my message?"

"Yes," I replied as well as I could; "but, you see, I fainted."

"Ah, yes," he cried in a kind of rage, "women usually do. But come along now," he continued, "for I've had him taken to his own house—that is, if your finer sensibilities can stand the sight," he finished with a sneer.

All this time it never had crossed my mind to find out how Paul had met his death. He was dead, and nothing else mattered. Martin, however, as we walked through the streets told me the whole story.

It seemed that Paul had bought some whiskey from a guide that they had with them, enough, in fact, to keep him in a drunken delirium for several days. Finally, when he had come to himself, he fell into a fit of despondency.

"I might almost call it acute melancholia," said Martin, "and he was far more depressed in spirits than after a drinking bout in the old days. I sat up half the night with him, trying to brace him up, and finally, thinking I had at last succeeded, I went to bed. Two hours later I awoke with the sound of a gunshot wringing in my ears. The guide and I ran out to find Paul lying dead before the fire, still grasping the barrel of his shot gun with an iron grip." He paused for a moment, and then went on again in his cold voice. "He had a whole in his side that you could stick your arm into," he finished.

I might as well say here that the story of the guide and the position of the body testified to the truth of Martin's account of the tragedy, and that at the coroner's inquest a verdict of suicide was immediately forthcoming.

Three days later Paul went to his last resting place. Browne, who had been a good friend to the boy, and occupied the same coach. It was one of those gray days in late autumn, when the rain falls drearily from the heavens, as though nature, now old and barren, were weeping over the wasteful abandonment of her youth.

Our snail's pace through the streets grated on my nerves, till I could have shouted to the man on the box, and told him to drive faster. All at once Browne's voice broke in upon my meditations.

"When a man takes a bitter dose of medicine he takes it in a hurry and doesn't sip it for the taste, does he?"

"No," I answered, at a loss for his meaning.

"Then why all this," and he pointed to his black clothes and then to mine, "and why is it we can't rattle along the stones at a faster pace?"

"Custom," I answered.

"Custom be damned, then," said he. "The natural, decent, sensible thing is to hide one's sacred inner feelings from the world, and not go parading it through the streets, as we are doing now, for the mob to jibber at. This is a relic of barbarism, and there goes another."

We were entering the cemetery as he spoke, and the first clang of the bell rang out in the still air.

"All this," he continued, "your friend Martin would very truly call the toys made for the mass mind. They are the things that hide a man's real feelings, and like wine intensify his emotions. But here we are, poor old Paul."

The vehicle came to a halt, and we got out. Soon a crowd had assembled, for Paul had had a host of friends, and the short service at the grave was well under way. Once I looked around, and saw Martin standing directly in back of me. I noticed his face was as expressionless as though it had been cut out of stone, and the eyes were fixed and were staring straight ahead at the coffin.

At last it was over, and the men were filling up the grave with earth so hardened with frost that each shovel-full fell on the lid of the casket with a dull thud. Then it was that I heard Martin speak, all unconsciously as it were.

"I have buried my heart with Paul," he said, but there was a strange exultation in his tone that did not tally with his words, and I saw Browne glance at him with a curious look.

X

Like clouds across a silver lake,
   The years roll by, are gone,
Upon our hearts reflections make
   Of troubles bravely borne.

Time works wonders with the heart of youth. Dearly
as I had loved my brother, each day took a little from
the load of my suffering, till gradually I fell back into the
grooves of everyday life again, and he became but a memory
to me, over which I lingered many a night by my lonely
fireside.

Martin had passed out of my life completely. Once I
read in the papers that he was working hard on a new book,
and one critic was courageous enough to say that, in his
opinion, Martin should have rested on his laurels, for to
bring out another volume of the same merit as his last was
well-nigh impossible. However that may be, I never saw the
man but once again, and that remains still to be told.

Browne became my best friend in the years that followed Paul's death, and he would drop in at the studio frequently for a chat and a smoke. He was a queer fellow, who could be intensely amusing at times. A sworn enemy to all conventionalities, be was a thorn in his fashionable mother's side, and many a tale he told me that would bring the tears to my eyes from laughter, of one of his wild crusades against the staid and established. Underneath all his eccentric ideas, as I deemed them, lay a good heart and a very shrewd brain. The condemnation of the man lay in the fact that he was immensely wealthy and constitutionally lazy.

Three years passed away, and then Martin's new book, that he had dedicated to my lost brother, appeared in print. If his first had caused a breeze of public comment, his last created a whirlwind. The title of this new work was The Confessions of Constantine. You, my readers, who have been fortunate or unfortunate enough to have read it before it was destroyed by the government, know those terrible sensations with which it inspired you. Sir Vivian Gerard aptly phrased it, in an article published in the *Colonial*, ending in these words: "I trembled when I read Many Murders, for those terrible crimes seemed to be pictured before my very eyes, but when I perused The Confessions of Constantine my hand was steady as I turned the pages, but in my brain was forming the blood lust of the murderer as he struck the fatal blow. I felt no repulsion at the savagery of it, but only the great unholy joy of brute rage and the love of killing. I cannot criticise this work, I can only wonder at it."

It was shortly after this book made its appearance, that the great wave of crime swept New York from end to end. The police force fought valiantly to hold it in check, but failed. In vain they made countless arrests, for still new murderers sprang up on all sides. It seemed as though it were a contagious disease, a murderer's microbe, as one learned fool maintained.

Just as things had reached such a climax that it was dangerous to go out alone at night unarmed, and the whole police force was in a frenzy of despair, a young man gained admittance to the station house and to the chief himself. He was a wealthy well-known young man named Browne, else he would have scarcely been received, for the chief of police had guarded himself like a feudal baron in his castle.

"Well," said he with a vigilant eye on Browne, "what is it?"

"I came," answered Browne, "about those murders that are happening so frequently of late."

"Well?" said the chief again.

"You want them stopped, don't you?" asked the young man simply.

Then, for the first time in many days, the chief laughed.

"Yes, I do," he said at length; "but how did you guess it?"

"In that case," said Browne coolly, "I can stop them, or, at least, the great majority."

For a moment the policeman looked at the young man with starting, vacant saucer eyes.

"How in hell—" he began, but the other interrupted him.

Stepping forward he pulled a book out of his pocket and presented it to the chief.

"You men of the police force know," he said, "that, as a rule, a disordered mind is responsible for murder. I went yesterday to the homes of the fifty murderers that were apprehended last week, seeking something, anything, that could create their mental frenzy. In forty-five of these homes I found that book, while in the remaining five, I discovered, it had been there, but after being read had been 'destroyed'. Are you familiar with the volume? It is called The Confessions of Constantine."

"No," replied the chief with knitted brows. "But what has that got to do with crime?" he continued. "Surely it was mere coincidence that they had the book, and nothing more."

"Maybe you are right," said Browne; "but read this short chapter, and then tell me how you feel."

The chief was impressed in spite of himself, and he glanced at the page that Browne indicated. Then, as my friend told me afterward, his eyes became fixed on the printed words, and the veins grew big and black on his forehead, while the knuckles in his hands stood out white from the grip he had on the arms of his chair. He read on and on, until at last Browne went up and touched him on the shoulder, and then he looked up with strange bloodshot eyes.

"What is it?" he asked thickly, and then before the other could answer he was himself again. "Good God, you're right!" he cried, springing to his feet. "I felt like a murderer just now myself."

"If it affects you that way, chief," said Browne, "imagine how it would affect a nervous, high-strung man who, perhaps, has an enemy, or, let us say, a dull brutal man with a wrong to avenge. It seems to me that it would overthrow the brain of the one for the time being, and feed the roaring beast in the other, till it would break through the bars of civilization, and feast itself in blood."

"You're right!" cried the chief again; "you're undoubtedly right. I can still feel the brute in me licking its lips. But what can we do?" he continued after a moment's pause. "The evil thing is scattered all over the world by now."

"That is your problem," answered Browne rising to his feet. "But if you want my advice, I would say, after you have proved my theory to be correct, that you appeal to those in authority to recall every copy of this book, and pay the standard price. They can be easily traced through the book stores. When you have collected them all, apply some kerosene and a match. Good day," and he was gone.

They acted on his advice. First, the prisoners were examined, and they all acknowledged reading the book and of being influenced by it. Next, they went to the government, and in the space of six months there were but two copies of this work in America—one in the Museum of Arts and Sciences, and the other in Browne's pocket. The chief of police got all the glory when the streets of the city were safe once more, but Browne was allowed to keep the book as a souvenir, and that was enough for him.

The book became his evil genius, but that must wait till another chapter.

XI

For it was a corpse forlorn,
With its hair and clothing torn,
And its life forever gone,
     Drifting by.

"I tell you the man is a menace to society, and should be exterminated, as though he were a poisonous snake writhing through the long grass."

It was Browne who had spoken. He had entered my studio a half hour before, with The Confessions of Constantine under his arm, and he had been reading passages of the condemned book aloud, while he railed at the author between breaths, as it were. I did not like his excited manner, and sought to soothe him.

"But he could hardly have guessed that his work would cause so much suffering and crime," I ventured.

"He couldn't, eh?" retorted Browne.

"Well, I think he could, and what's more, I'm sure of it. A great genius never underestimates himself or his work, and a man, who could write like that, could readily understand the effect it would have on his readers. Why, I believe he planned it."

"Oh, come now," I broke in, "that's a little bit too much."

"Not at all," he cried in excitement, "not at all. Any man who could formulate such horrible thoughts in his brain, and who had such a terrible imagination as Martin's book indicates, would delight in the results. Each murder would add a leaf in his wreathe of glory, and whisper in his ear that he alone was master of his art. I can see him now, reading the grewsome headlines in the paper, and chuckling over them like some black devil in hell, while he mutters to himself, 'This, all this, is my work'—"

He stopped for breath, and I noticed that his heightened color and flashing eyes indicated an unhealthy excitement, entirely foreign to the man. Again I sought to pacify him.

"I think you do Martin an injustice," I said. "He told me himself, when we were in Paris together, that he had never had any imagination at all, so he probably gets his stories from the roughs on the East Side."

"No imagination?" he faltered. "No imagination?"

"No," I replied; "he clearly told me that he hadn't."

"Then, how does he describe the sensations in the brain of the murderer, as he does so plainly in that?" he demanded, and he pointed to the book.

"Some one told him about them, I suppose," I answered.

He threw back his head and laughed a harsh, grating laugh.

"It must have been a second Martin, then," said he, after a short pause, "for feelings, such as those must be, are hard to describe exactly as they are, and harder yet to remember."

He was silent for some time after this, evidently thinking deeply.

"Have you his first book," he asked suddenly.

I nodded an assent, and going over to the bookcase, returned with Many Murders in my hand. He took it from me, and opened it at random. He started reading it to himself, and then shutting it abruptly, opened his own copy of The Confessions of Constantine. He seemed to be comparing the two. Finally, he spoke again.

"This came out before Paul's death, didn't it?" and he held up Many Murders.

"Yes," I answered, entirely at a loss for his meaning.

"Then," said he, "I think the world can have but little more to fear from the Mysterious Martin," and he rose to his feet.

Just at this moment there came a knock upon the door. It was a messenger boy who entered.

"Is there a Mr. George Browne here," he asked.

"I'm the man," answered Browne, stepping forward.

"Well, here's a registered letter for you, sir. I was around to your flat," he continued, "but your man says you ain't in, and puts me wise to this joint, so I comes here, thinking it might be important."

Browne put an end to his conversation with a half dollar, and the boy, with a hurried, "Thank you, Mister," was gone, thinking, no doubt, that the gentleman might repent of his generosity, and want it back again.

Browne, opening the letter, read its contents, and, with a black look, passed it to me. It was but of three or four lines, and read thus:

MY DEAR BROWNE: I hear that you have become quite a critic recently, and, in the case of my last book, a very stern one. I have now finished another tale, which I wish you would criticise, this time before I submit it to the world, so that it will not meet with the same fate as that other. I will be home at eight o'clock to-night, and hope that you will do me the honor to call.

Sincerely yours,

S. MARTIN.

"Are you going?" I asked, handing it back.

"Yes," he answered, "and with a stronger belief than ever that it would be a God send to strike this creature down, and with some hope now that I will be able to do it."

He left me in a bewildered state. Could his mind be giving way by too much reading of that terrible book, I wondered, and the thought worried me the entire afternoon.

A week passed, and I saw nothing of Browne. This was very unusual, for scarcely a day had gone by for many months that he hadn't dropped in to see me. Vague misgivings, of I knew not what, oppressed me constantly. On the eighth day I decided to look him up, and had started descending the stairs to the street, when I came face to face with a little dark man coming up.

"Are you Mr. Smithers?" said he.

"Yes," I said in surprise. "What can I do for you?"

"I want a few minutes of your time," he replied. "To ask you about a friend of yours."

"Certainly," I answered. "What is it?"

"It's about a man named Browne," he continued slowly, "and I think we had better have our little talk in your studio."

I led the way back to the room with my brain awhirl. The man gave me no time to compose myself. No sooner had the door closed behind us than he spoke, regarding me fixedly the while.

"I understand that Browne was here the afternoon of the twenty-fifth?" said he.

"Yes," I cried; "but why—"

"Oh, I'm Green of the detective bureau," he broke in, and he opened his coat and showed me his badge. "You see," he continued, "the man's been missing for over a week now, and his mother has put the thing in the hands of the police. When last seen he was leaving this place, and we thought that you might be able to give us a little information—where he intended going that night, for instance, or any thing of that kind."

Then I did a thing that I have regretted bitterly ever since. I can only lay the blame on the excited condition that I was in, that seemed to paralyze what little thinking ability I had, and that made me answer his questions like a child. I told him everything, of the letter that Browne had received, and of his threatening words in regard to Martin, and he thanked me profusely as he started to leave.

"Mr. Smithers," said he, "if other people were as willing to give evidence as you are, why, the work of a detective would dwindle down to nothing. By the way," he continued at the door, "Martin has also disappeared, and, from what you have said, it would seem that, could we find Browne, he would know a little about the disappearance of the author."

Then, when he had gone, it flashed through my benumbed brain what I had done. I had branded my own friend as a murderer, and had slipped the halter about his neck. I realized for the first time the frightful significance of his threatening words, when speaking of Martin, coupled with the disappearance of the two men. Yes, I had made an ass of myself, and the only thing left to me now was to sit down and await results, I thought, and then, after all, the whole thing might be foolishness, and both men turn up hale and hearty. It is human to hope for the best.

Days turned into weeks, but still nothing was heard of the missing men. The newspapers took it up, and it became the sensation of the year. It was remembered that Browne had had Martin's book condemned by the government, and, from this fact, a long-standing grudge between the two men was more than hinted at. Then came wild conjectures of possible duels to the death, and suicide pacts.

Finally, a full month after the detective had visited me, a body was found floating down the East River. The face and head of the corpse had been beaten to a jelly by some heavy weapon, while its body had been so disfigured by its long submersion in the water that it was impossible to recognize it, except for a ring that it had on its swollen finger, on which was ingraved the two letters, S and M.

That night the news went through the city that Martin's remains had been discovered. The following day the thing be came a certainty, for the little tailor, who had made Martin's clothes for years, went to the morgue and recognized the ragged suit that the corpse had worn as one that he had made for the author two months before.

If Martin had been murdered, as was evidently the case, what had become of his companion, Browne, on the night that they had both disappeared? Was the latter guilty of the author's death, and if he was not, why did he not come forward and prove it? Questions like these appeared in all the leading magazines and newspapers, but still the missing man remained missing, and the riddle was no nearer its solution than before. Finally an article, written by the chief of police, appeared in the daily *Gazette*. It gave my interview with the detective word for word, and ended by saying the following:

"Mr. Browne, after saving the city from a thousand crimes, failed to take his own cure, and fell a victim to a brain malady from which he had rescued so many others."

After this came out, there could be but one verdict: The world remembered George Browne as a murderer and a mad man.

XII

A soft wind is gently playing
    With the eyelids of the morn,
While the hounds are loudly baying
    At the moon, now cold, forlorn.

Years passed by, and still George Browne was among the missing. It was as though he had vanished into thin air, and although the shrewdest detectives of the continent took up the case, they worked in vain. No clue of the slightest kind was forthcoming, and so gradually, one by one, they gave up, and went back to the solving of less difficult problems. Soon new sensations arose that drew the interest of the public, and the whole affair became well-nigh forgotten.

It is not my purpose to dwell too closely on the years that followed. Suffice it to say, that they brought me wealth, distinction, and the respect of all. What a pitifully empty thing is this same respect of the mob, when one cannot respect oneself. It would be unbearable were it not so ludicrous. Sometimes it gave me a bitter pleasure to think how I had sold the public, and then the thought would steal into my brain, that perhaps I had not sold the public, but, in reality, had sold myself. At those times I was a very unhappy man.

Twenty years after the events recorded in the preceding chapter, I laid aside my brush forever. I was now fifty years of age, and a very wealthy man, yet my health was not what it should have been. I consulted a physician, and he advised me to take a trip to the Maine woods for a month or so. Stuart, a friend of mine, promised to accompany me, but at the last moment, an important business affair interfered, and kept him in town a week later than he had expected. As my preparations for the trip were all made, I decided not to wait for him, but to go up alone. He recommended a place, and said that he would meet me there in a week's time.

"By the way," he said as we parted at the station, "don't forget to hire Bill Pete when you get to the hotel. He's the best guide in the business, and can show you some fine hunting and fishing."

"I won't," I answered as I boarded the train.

The trip was an uneventful one, and ended by a ten-mile drive from the station to the hotel. This stood on the banks of a little lake, and was the only human habitation for many a wild forest mile of underbrush. The latent love for the beautiful that was a part of me, warmed to the majestic scenery, stretching away on every side. The hills, with their virgin timber, invited exploration, while the placid sheet of water seemed to hide a thousand world old secrets.

The place at that time was little known, and on this account there were scarcely a dozen people beside myself in the dining room. Immediately after dinner, I made inquiries regarding the guide, Bill Pete.

"No, he's not here now," said the little bald man behind the desk, "but he's liable to drop in most any minute, and when he does I'll send him to you."

A few minutes later I was sitting on the veranda, with a cigar between my lips. The moon by now was rising slowly over the black tree-trunks, a round blood-red ball of fire, that gradually, as it ascended higher in the heavens, lost its vivid coloring, and became a pale silver, while the water, under its magic touch, changed to a sea of dancing light.

"How beautiful it is," I murmured half aloud.

"Yes," said a voice beside me, "beautiful it may be, but it is horrible as well."

I started in surprise, not so much from the strange words as from the tone of the voice in which they were spoken. I have heard that man speak before, I thought, but where and when? I puzzled my brains in vain, the answer was not forthcoming, and my eyes could make out nothing in the gloom, except that, as he stood beside me, he looked tall and slender.

"Horrible?" I repeated slowly. "How is it horrible?"

"Look," he cried, and he pointed upward to the sky, "that smile upon the moon's face is no smile, but a grimace of terror like one sees on a death's head, when the jaw drops down, and see how pale, how very pale it is. A thin, dead face is a natural thing, but a round, bloated one is horrible."

He paused for a moment, and then went on once more.

"It is as though nature had planted a death's head there in the sky," he continued quietly, "to warn mankind that no life can live forever, or it may be as a puzzle to the world, to answer which one cannot be of this world, namely, what is death and the sensation of dying. The human race cares nothing for this question. They hide it from themselves, and disguise it under many different masks. They play with the moon as a baby might play with the face of its death mother. They even write songs about it, and call it the jolly, smiling moon, while all the years that great white face looks down upon them in frozen horror."

He had seemed to have been talking to himself rather than to me, and his voice still had that familiar ring to it. I could master my curiosity no longer.

"I must have met you somewhere before," I broke in.

"I rather think not," said he. "My name is Bill Pete."

"Not the guide?" I cried.

"The very same," he responded. "I heard you were looking for a guide, and so I came out here to see if I wouldn't do. The people in the hotel will tell you that I know the woods pretty well in these parts, and that I have a snug little cabin across the lake, if you were thinking of camping out."

All the refinement died out of his voice as he told me who he was, and it was as though he were a different man who was speaking.

XIII

Oh, whispering tales, that the night breezes
   blow,
That sighing and dying and echoing low,
From the listening, glistening moon gently
   flow
       In the dark.

For the next few days Bill Pete was my constant companion. The morning after our talk, he paddled me across the lake, with the deft silent strokes of an Indian. Sitting in the bow of the canoe, facing him, I made the best of my opportunity to study his countenance, for I still had the impression, that somewhere at some time I had met the man before. This feeling grew stronger with me each moment, yet for the life of me I couldn't tell why. The guide's thin face, heavily bearded and bronzed well-nigh to a copper color, certainly was not familiar to me, while his eyes were completely concealed by a pair of blue eye-glasses, yet for all that, lurking somewhere, it might be in the very inner being of the man, was something that struck a long disused discordant note in my own breast. I had a strange feeling that behind those heavy glasses lay the answer to the riddle, and for one insane moment I was strongly tempted to spring forward and jerk them off his nose, but luckily I restrained myself.

"Tell me," I said at length, "why do you wear those things?"

"What things?" he asked blankly, and, although his face was half turned from me, I felt instinctively that he was gazing at me intently.

"Why, those glasses, of course," I cried testily.

"My eyes are very weak," he answered and then lapsed into silence again.

Not another word was said until we had landed on the other shore, and then, after dragging the canoe up on the tiny beach, Bill Pete showed me his cabin.

It was the usual affair, built of logs, and containing four bunks, filled with the sweet-smelling pine boughs. The hut boasted of a roughly constructed table, some pots and pans hung upon the wall, a stove in one corner, and a doorway, but no vestige of a door. This last omission bothered me a trifle, but I was soon to learn that the only wild animal that availed himself of it, was the hedgehog, the glutton of the forest. In front, barely a hundred feet from the doorway, the water rippled on the beach, while behind lay the great expanse of forest.

Bill Pete proved to be a very silent man, speaking rarely and then always to the point, while a smile never brightened his sombre expression. Although he was a poor companion, he proved to be an excellent guide, and seemed to know the woods like the very creatures of the woods. His tread was as noiseless as a cat, and I have seen him creep up within a dozen feet of a feeding deer before the animal sprang away in fright. He knew where the best fishing could be found, and, taking his advice, I had great luck with the rod. Soon, less than a week had passed by, I felt a different man from the broken-down artist who had left New York under the doctor's orders.

This brings me up to the night of the fourteenth of July. Even now, after so many years have gone their way, my hand still trembles, as I write these words, for the horror of those fearful hours is upon me yet. It is, thank God, the lot of very few to see a black soul stripped bare and writhing out its life alone.

It had been a hard day's tramp through the forest, and I was deliciously tired, as I lay before the open fire, gazing out into the gloom beyond. Bill Pete sat a few feet from me, his pipe between his teeth, and his sombre face in the shadow. The wind had been rising steadily for an hour, and now I could hear, every now and then, a distant growl of thunder. In the eddying gusts of the breeze, the fire would spring up fiercely, and, as the flames shone brighter, the tree-trunks would seem to leap forward out of the darkness, like live things, and fly back again as though in fright when the light sank lower once more.

"It looks like a stormy night," I ventured at last.

Bill Pete nodded his head in assent, but said never a word. Again there was silence, except for the moaning of the wind through the tossing branches of the pine-trees overhead.

"Stuart will be here to-morrow," I said in a desperate effort to make the man speak. "Do you know him?"

Again my taciturn companion merely nodded his head in answer.

"By Jove!" I cried in irritation, "you remind me of a man I used to know a good many years ago."

"Who was that?" said the guide so quickly that I was taken aback for the moment, and had all I could do to answer him immediately.

"A man by the name of Martin," I answered in surprise, for it was the first time that he had spoken the whole day through.

Snap went something that sounded like a dry twig, and looking across at Bill Pete I saw the red glowing bowl of his pipe beside his foot. He had bitten through the stem, and spat out the broken piece of it before he spoke again.

"And what became of this Martin?" he asked in a strained, husky voice.

"Why, you must know," I replied. "He was that famous author who was murdered about twenty years ago. Surely you remember that?"

"Now you speak of it, I do seem to remember something of the case," said he, "but in what way do I remind you of him."

"Your silence," I said.

"My silence?" he repeated.

"Yes," I answered. "Martin seemed to begrudge a man every word he used in speaking to that man, and you appear to be the same way."

"Oh, is that all!" he cried in a tone of relief, and relapsed into silence once more.

Finally I got to my feet with a yawn, and, with a last glance at the shadows that played among the tree-trunks, went inside the cabin, leaving Bill Pete still sitting beside the fire, evidently lost in a deep revery.

In a few minutes more I had crawled into my sleeping bag, and was wrapt in an oblivion of slumber. How long I slept I do not know, but this I know, that I awoke trembling in every limb, with some thing cold and clammy on my forehead, something that might have been a lizard or a toad, or even the hand of a dead man.

As my eyes opened, I saw, bending over me, the dark shape of a man, but in the uncertain light of the room, the lantern had been turned low, I could make out nothing more. I attempted to rise in my bunk, and found that I had been tied securely to it, so that I was held motionless, although I could move my head from side to side.

Still the dim shape stood beside me with its cold hand upon my brow. Under its touch I felt my flesh quivering in repulsion, and the blood freezing in my veins.

"Who are you?" I gasped. "Who are you?"

As though in answer the light flared up on a sudden, and I saw the cruel, thin face and the burning gray eyes of the murdered Martin, like a horrible nightmare, bending down nearer and nearer, as though he would gaze into my very soul.

XIV

But, see, a scintillating light
    Awakes my dormant brain;
Resplendent self before my sight
    Has shaken off the chain.

There is no fear like the fear of the supernatural. When the mind cannot explain, when the brain itself is paralyzed and frozen from fright, that indeed is terrible.

Here, in this dimly lighted room, shut off from the world, I was looking into the face of a man, who, to my own knowledge, had been murdered and buried twenty years before, and so was it any wonder that I felt my reason giving way under the strain of it. Yet, in spite of my condition and the fact that my eyes never left that terrible face above me, I was conscious, in some uncanny way, of the objects immediately surrounding me. For example, I felt instinctively that a blanket had been fastened across the doorway to keep out the wind, which now howled in baffled fury about the cabin, yet I had not glanced that way, not even for the fraction of a second. The long-threatening storm had risen while I slept, and was now breaking from the heavens in a deluge of rain, and peel after peel of crashing thunder. In that first awful moment I tried to cry out, but my tongue clove to the roof of my mouth, and my throat was as dry as tinder, and thus I remained all those weary hours, as mute as a new-born child.

"You are wrong, Smithers," said the voice above me, "for I am no ghost, but I am what is far more to be feared, for, if there are such things as spirits of the dead, I have created a hundred, nay, a thousand."

There was a silence for a moment, interrupted only by the howling of the wind, and then again the voice went on wearily monotonously:

"The story of my life, which I am about to tell, you will think but one long, red line of wanton cruelty and mad blood lust, but underneath it all is the thread that you will miss, namely, the great sacrifice of a strong nature to kindle the immortal flame of genius and create the indestructible. Why do I tell you this? Because of the world you are truly worldly, and therefore a fit messenger to carry my words to all mankind."

Again he paused for a moment, and then went on more hurriedly, as though time were a very precious thing indeed.

"I remember that I told you of my mother and father's death," he continued, "and that a great-aunt adopted me and drummed spiritualism into my childish ears. In that great, gloomy house of hers the books were my only companions, and what a collection there were. The Mysteries of Paris was there and also The Tales of the

Bastile, and a score of other horror stories, but how I loved them all, and how I lingered over them from early dawn till late at night, forgetting time, place, and the very functions of life in the contemplation of them.

Gradually a great ambition began to take form within me. Why could not I write like this someday, or, who could tell, perhaps even better? Everything was possible, and why should I not succeed, I, Sterling Martin, if I gave my life to it? When I asked myself this question, a voice within me seemed to answer.

"You will succeed, and you cast your mortal side behind you," it cried. "Tear out your heart and your head will rise above the stars."

The meaning of this was lost upon me for the time, but I was soon to learn.

One day I sat down hopefully, with paper and pencil in my hands, to begin my career, to write a horror story. From the first, the horrible in literature was the thing that held me, and so it was but natural that I should devote my own efforts to the same strain. For over an hour I sat there motionless, the paper on my knee and the pencil idle in my fingers. Then, all at once, the sickening truth overpowered me, and I broke down like a nervous woman and wept bitterly.

I was in a worse position than a sailor without a ship, or a girl without a sweetheart, for I was a writer without an imagination.

No doubt my literary career would have been ended then, before it had begun, had not an unlooked-for accident occurred that very night, and at almost that exact moment.

My aunt had been very sick for over a week, and now was dying upstairs in her large, old-fashioned bed. As I sat

with the weak tears running down my face, there came a
gentle rap on the door. It was an old servant who had come
to take me to the sick room for a last look at the dying
woman.

When I entered my aunt was almost at her last gasp.
Her long yellow hands, like the leaves of Autumn, were
fluttering about the coverlet, while the death-rattle rasped
harshly in her weazened throat. Soon it was all over, and
they had closed the blue-veined eyelids forever. Then the
nurse turned to me, and, seeing the mark of tears on my
cheeks, not knowing the true reason for them, bustled me
out of the room with, "There, there, child, don't cry," and a
pat on the shoulder.

All the way back to the library I seemed to see the
death-bed scene and nothing else. It was as though it were
painted on the walls and ceilings in glowing colors, and
hiding in the corners where the shadows played.

There, lying on the chair, where I had left them, were
my discarded paper and pencil. Picking them up, half
unconsciously, I started to write, as it were in a dream, while
ever before my eyes was the mental picture of the dying
woman gasping for breath.

How long this strange mental state possessed me, I had
no means of ascertaining, but I know, that at last, it fled like
a mist before the breeze, and that then I was myself once
more.

I still held the piece of paper in my hand, only now,
instead of being a plain blank sheet, it was covered on both
sides with writing, my writing. Slowly I read it aloud, while
a great living joy sprang up in my heart, for the thing was a
masterpiece. It was a description of a deathbed scene such
as I had just witnessed, but so realistic and of such perfect

wording that it was as though the scene were being enacted before one's eyes.

"Could this be mine?" I asked myself.

Yes, I concluded, it is mine, for the writing is my writing, and the description is the description of what I have just seen.

Then I cried aloud in triumph, "This is the work of a great writer, and the echoes in the silent house brought back my words as though in answer, "This is the work of a great writer." That night, at the age of fourteen, I laid the foundations for my future life.

"I have no imagination," I said to myself, "therefore I can only describe what I see with my own eyes, and what I hear with my own ears. The horrible appeals to me, and to that theme I shall devote myself. On this account, I must steel my heart against all feelings of pity and compassion, because to see and hear the terrible, I must witness the perpetration of crime, and it may be even aid and abet a murderer to create my model for me. I must associate with the scum of the earth, to rise above the world. I must tear out of my being all human feeling, to become superhuman. In other words, I must become a heartless brute to reach my goal, the summit of literary fame."

All this I realized, and yet I did not turn back.

Far in front of me, in my dreams that night, I seemed to see a throne and a scepter, toward which I was being carried swiftly by a great multitude. I felt that this was my day of triumph, and that the throne and scepter should be mine, yet those who carried me said never a word, but were as silent as spectres. Suddenly a terrible thought crossed my mind. It might be that these were not living men at all. At that moment they fell down in long, straight lines, and gazed up to the pale sky with glassy eyes, leaving me standing there alone, hemmed in by death.

I awoke, bathed in cold sweat from head to foot.

His next few words were lost upon me, swallowed up as they were by a crash of thunder that seemed to shake the cabin till the pots and pans rattled on the wall.

XV

When the works no longer run,
Have we stopped or just begun?
By life is it rest we've won
    Forever?

"For many months," resumed the voice, "I trained myself for the career I had chosen, killing off my human virtues one by one, and thus gradually molding myself into a heartless machine. This, I knew from the first, was absolutely necessary to insure my success.

As I have already said, up to that point in my life, I had had little or no intercourse with my fellow men, shut off from the world as I was, and in consequence of this I was absolutely devoid of all feeling for others. All the strong love of my nature was centred on the dumb animals about me. Even the very mice in the wall knew me for their friend, and they would come out of their hiding places, while I was in the library alone, and scamper over my feet, so fearless were they.

Now I had to go through the first great sacrifice for my art. "Tear out your heart, and your head will rise above the stars," I told myself, and then there remained but the one thing for me to do.

Coldly, methodically, but with, oh, what mental anguish, I tortured to death each one of my dumb animal friends that I had loved so. My brain reeled, but my hand was steady, and after each atrocious act, I felt the natural repulsion and horror for my cruelties growing less and less. I was slowly conquering myself. The diary, I kept at that time, describing my different emotions, still causes me to tremble as I glance over it, for it pictures before me vividly the acute sufferings of my youth.

At about that period in my life, I noticed in a general way, that the illustrations in a great book often did more to mar it than the pen of the most bitter critic could do, and so I decided to teach myself to draw and paint, so as to do justice to my own writing at least.

This came very easily, for when my model was death in any form, I had but to sit down before it with a paper and pencil, and then, in a moment, I was in a kind of mental daze, from which I would awake to find that I had created a most striking realistic likeness of the scene before me. This condition of mind was almost identically the same as I experienced while writing.

I now considered myself prepared for a broader field of action, so I entered a school in a town nearby, more in a search for the sensational than for any knowledge they could teach me. Here the months dragged away wearily, however, and nothing happened of interest.

Finally, I had about decided to create my own horror, when, leaving the schoolhouse one afternoon, I saw something that drew my attention. This was nothing more nor less than a girl, who was in my own class, walking down the street with an overgrown lad, whose vacant eye and moving lips indicated a weak mind if not actual idiocy. I made inquiries, and discovered that this half-witted fool lived near the girl, and that he would often carry her books home from the village. That very night I decided upon a plan that later proved entirely successful.

The next day I won the affections of the poor idiot by some small kindness, and ascertained that a certain theory of mine was correct. The poor fellow could not think, but he could love, as only a much abused outcast can love. The rest you have read in the Murder of Mary Mortimer.

I was that voice that drove the poor idiot on, that voice which turned the love in his undeveloped nature to a seething inferno of jealous hatred. I drove him to his crime, and watched him as he slit the girl's throat from ear to ear, then I made a sketch of her as she lay dead in the discolored snow.

To say that I felt no compassion for her would be to tell a lie. A dozen times I was on the point of leaping out of the underbrush, where I had concealed myself , to save her before it was too late, but each time, just as I was about to do so, a voice seemed to whisper in my ear.

"Fool," it said, "tear out your heart, and your head will rise above the stars."

Then I forced myself to remain there in hiding, and my first great battle was won.

When the girl was lifeless, strange to say, all my feelings of compassion vanished, and I strode out coolly to where she lay in an ever-widening bloody stain, and drawing out my paper and pencil, which I had brought for that purpose, drew a picture of her. I was all alone while I worked, for the idiot had fled immediately after the crime, and I remember that it pleased me. Finally, I plodded home, still in the mental daze of creation, and quite unconscious of the snow that beat against my upturned face.

Again the voice stopped, and waited for a reverberating peel of thunder to die away, before it continued, while I, speechless from horror, felt my head shaking violently from side to side, as though I had the palsy.

"Now I come to your brother, Smithers," it went on grimly. You, who have shared your affections with the mob, can scarcely understand the feeling I had for him. He was wife, brother and friend to me, the personification of all my earthly love. He was the good in me, that I had torn from my being, and, when I was with him, I felt my old strangled emotions coming to life again.

All this I fought against, knowing it to be foolish weakness, but it was in vain, I was powerless.

Then came the years in Paris, and still I could not forget. The flame of human feeling that he had kindled in my breast burnt on and on, and would not be extinguished. I, who as a mere boy, had caused a frightful murder to be committed, now could scarcely enter the morgue without a feeling of compassion and horror.

What would become of my art, I thought. Would all my sacrifice and crime be for naught? Yes, all wasted, my reason answered, unless you can conquer yourself once more. Then I plunged into my work furiously, for it was thus alone that I could forget myself.

Finally, I heard that Paul was drinking again, and fearing that he might take his own life in one of his strange fits of depression, I went back to America, and straightened him out in no time. This I acknowledged to myself as weakness, but although I struggled against it, nevertheless, it conquered me.

Then I engaged lodgings in one of the slums of New York, for I intended making one last fight for my career, and was soon hand-in-glove with a gang of criminals, composed, for the most part, of men who would willingly slice a throat for a five-dollar bill. Surprising as it may seem there are hundreds like that in any great city.

Under my skilled leadership a dozen murders were committed with no one the wiser. Our victims were poor rum-soaked derelicts, whose disappearance from the world was not even noted, and if it had been, would have caused very little comment and therefore no danger of detection.

I witnessed every one of these crimes, and they are recorded faithfully in my book entitled Many Murders, yet each killing I saw was a torture to me, and the remorse I suffered afterward was almost more than I could bear. I avoided Paul as much as possible during these months, for in his presence I felt like the cowering prisoner must feel before his executioner.

My first book was a success, but a disappointment to me. It was all very well in its small way, but I had not gone deep enough into my subject. How could I improve on it with my next, I wondered, and then like a flash the idea came to me. Before I had described the crime from the standpoint of the onlooker, the usual common way, but in my work henceforth I would go far deeper, and give the feelings of the murderer, as he struck the fatal blow.

This would be unique in literature, for I would not guess at nor imagine those feelings, but I would commit murder myself, and thus know.

Three days after I had come to this decision, I tried to kill a man in my room. He had been drugged in the saloon below, and then dragged in by two of my villainous associates. He was lying unconscious on the bed, and I was alone with him. Stealing up beside him, I poised the knife in the air above his heart. All I had to do was to drop my arm, and he would have been a corpse, yet, try as I would, this simple action was beyond me. I thought I saw a resemblance to Paul in his white upturned face, and then I threw the knife upon the floor, and fell on my knees beside the bed, shaking all over with hysterical sobs. You see, I was still a very human man.

That night a great and final battle went on within me. At first Paul and my better self would gain the ascendency, then would come my art and the machine that I had made of myself to take its place. Thus it went, all through the dark hours, neither side gaining the advantage, but just as the gray of dawn had touched the city I had made up my mind.

"I must sever the last link that holds me to humanity," I cried in an awful voice that echoed strangely in my own ears. "Paul must be sacrificed, yes, as others have been sacrificed on the funeral pile of genius. Others have starved for it, and shall I turn back. Others have forfeited their loved ones because of it, and shall I be weak? No, Paul, my dear friend, you must die."

Three weeks later we were together in the Maine woods.

"Have a drink, Paul," I said, and passed him a flask of whiskey.

"But," he answered, "you know I'm off the stuff."

"Oh, that's when you're in town," I cried. "Surely a drink won't hurt you. When you get back, why go on the wagon again."

He fluttered about the whiskey for a few moments, like a moth around a candle, and then, like the moth, took the fatal plunge.

For two whole days I kept him in a drunken stupor by passing him the bottle whenever he showed signs of returning reason, and then quite suddenly I stopped. When he came to himself he was in a mood of the deepest depression, which gradually took the form of violent melancholia. Heartily sick in body, he was sicker yet in mind.

"I wish to God I were dead," he cried, turning toward me with a feverish light in his eyes.

"It would be a very good thing if you were," I retorted brutally. "Yes," I continued with a breaking heart, "for you are a drunkard, and can never be anything but a drunkard. A menace to society, a running sore on the face of the earth, you will die in the gutter, a disgrace to your brother and everybody else that knows you. Indeed, you had better die."

"Do you mean that," said he, with the feverish light now fairly blazing in his bloodshot eyes.

"I surely do," I answered very slowly and distinctly. "And, what's more," I added, "the sooner the better."

Mental depression following a debauch is a terrible thing even when we have friends to cheer us up, but in Paul's case, I had turned his mind into a seething hell. When I had left him by the fireside alone I knew what I had done only too well, and I suffered in the silent cabin as, even I, had never suffered before. How I envied the sleeping guide that moment, his unconsciousness, and how I prayed that the thing would happen quickly, and end my torment forever.

Suddenly I saw a hand slide through the open doorway and clutch the barrel of a gun that stood against the wall, then the weapon vanished as though by magic. I seized the sides of the bunk in which I was lying, and practically held myself motionless in that terrible moment.

"Only a moment now," I gasped to myself, "only a moment," and then there came the report of a gun, while something snapped in my brain that left me as cold and unfeeling as a man of stone.

"What is the use of my going out to look?" I muttered, as the guide disappeared through the doorway, "I know that he is dead without that."

The man came back instantly, with his face as white as chalk in the early morning light.

"Mr. Martin," he cried hoarsely, "Mr. Martin, he's shot himself."

"Indeed?" said I, and rolling over on my side I went fast to sleep like a little child.

XVI

So now I hear you gently sigh
Where will go to when I die;
Will I go on then, bye and bye,
    You who know?

When returned to New York, I immediately started
gathering material for my new book. Patiently and cleverly
I arranged a murder, in which I took the main rôle, and
did the actual killing myself for the first time. Since the
death of Paul I had been a man absolutely heartless, and in
consequence I committed the crime without the slightest
hesitation, and the story of it, describing my sensations
in a most minute manner, you have probably read in The
Confessions of Constantine.

In the course of the three years that followed, I
committed twelve crimes in all. I could have murdered far
more than that had I been actuated by the love of killing
alone, but this was not the case. I destroyed life merely for

my art's sake, and had no wish to be a wholesale butcher, for, if I killed wantonly to any great extent, I was afraid that my nerves would lose their high tension, and thus the sensations of the murderer would be dulled.

When my book came out, I said to myself: "Now for the greatest test of all." I was not mistaken in the quality of my work, and the great flood of crime that swept New York was praise enough for me. I had not only appealed to the mind of my weaker readers, but I had conquered their minds. I was the maker of men's destinies, the angel of death. The frail might succumb to my will and perish, but the strong became but the stronger, and went on unafraid. Just at this time, when the world seemed mine to play with and excite to any whim that pleased me, the roof of the heavens f ell upon my head, The Confessions of Constantine was condemned by the government.

In a very short time I had found out who was responsible for my downfall, and I, who had known but one human feeling, now was plunged into a very abyss of hate.

I did not underestimate George Browne for a moment. He was an individualist, and clever past belief. The man had already put two and two together, and was he not soon to put four and four together as well, I asked myself? He would be comparing my two books, I thought, and then he will begin to suspect the truth.

I immediately wrote him a letter, and in it asked him to see me that very day, as I had something that I wanted him to criticise. Then I made my plans. He was the stone in my path that had tripped me up, the mote in my eye that threatened to blind me, I must destroy him.

I concealed three of my brutal associates in the heavy curtains of the bedroom, and awaited his coming impatiently. At last I heard his knock upon the door.

"Come in!" I cried, and the man stood before me.

He was very pale, and I noticed a subdued excitement about him that made me very glad that I had taken such careful precautions. Then I rose to my feet, and offered to shake his hand.

"No, thank you," he cried, stepping back, "I don't shake hands with a murderer."

At that I realized that he had already put four and four together.

"How did you find it out so soon," I asked him quite simply.

He was strangely taken aback by my question, and I saw a puzzled look creep up into his eyes.

"Then you confess," he faltered at last.

"Certainly," I answered. "Why shouldn't I?" and I raised my hand above my head.

The signal had been given, and the three ruffians leaped from their hiding place. In a moment more Browne was overpowered and bound hand and foot. Then I looked into his face again, hoping to find fear written there. I was sorely disappointed. It was true, the perplexed look was gone, but in its place burned the flame of a great heroism and fortitude.

"I was at a loss for your meaning at first," he said in a quiet voice, and I bowed a silent assent. "You are going to kill me, of course?" he added.

"We are most certainly going to kill you," I replied.

"Then hear me," he broke in with excitement. "I want to speak to you of your literature, of your art."

"Yes?" I said.

"You have described crime," he continued rapidly, "from the standpoint of the onlooker, of the murderer, but the most horrible situation and, therefore, the most artistic, you have missed altogether."

"And what is that?" I asked with surprise.

"Why, the standpoint of the victim, of course," he cried, "or, in other words, what is the exact sensation of death."

"What is the exact sensation of death?" I repeated dully.

"Yes, that's it!" he shouted almost gleefully. "You're worse than a failure, Martin, for you're only a partial success. You, they call the recorder of sensations, have missed the unknown sensation, the one great mysterious sensation of death. Till you have mastered that you're a living lie. I will know that secret, and you will see its mystery in my dead eyes, and I will laugh ha! ha! for I will know more than the Mysterious Martin."

Then a terrible rage seized me, and, grasping an iron poker in my hand, I cracked his skull as though it had been an eggshell, and he fell down before me, dead, with the smile still upon his lips.

What was the sensation of death, I wondered, as I gazed down at the corpse that I had made. Here was one who knew, I thought, and again rage overmastered me, so that I beat the dead face into an unrecognizable bloody pulp. At that moment an idea occurred to me that made me chuckle aloud, for I had noticed that Browne had been a man of my own height.

I had the clothes stripped from the dead body, and an old suit of mine put on it, and then I slipped an initial ring, that I had worn for many years, on the cold hand of the corpse.

I commanded my associates to drop the battered thing into the river by stealth, and giving each of them a little hush money, so that they might carry out my instructions the more carefully, I left my room for the last time and incidentally the city. At first I fled to Canada, where I grew a beard and adopted the wearing of colored eyeglasses as a disguise. Here I read the New York papers with the keenest delight, to see that it was as I had planned, and that the world looked upon me as a dead genius, while the memory of Browne was stained with murder.

The voice was still for a moment, but when began again it was hoarse from long-suppressed emotion.

"But that was such a long time ago," it continued. "Nothing amuses me now—nothing. For twenty long years the question, what is the sensation of death, has driven me well-nigh mad, indeed, the world would think me mad, but the moon knows better. Last night, as the awful question was pounding in my brain, she, who knows all, bent her round, dead face beside me, and whispered to me, telling me how I could learn, and be as wise as she and other cold things. Ho! ho! ho! just think, to be as wise as the moon, who sees everything, for I'll know the exact sensations of death.

No wonder Browne laughed when I smashed his brains out, for he was wise, too—very wise."

Again the shrill laughter of the madman mingled with the howling of the gale till it sounded in my ears as though every devil in hell were screaming in frightful merriment.

XVII

I am weary, oh my God, I am weary.
The tide of life runs slow,
I'd not watch its icy flow.
Let me go, let me go,
    I am weary.

"How long I have waited. God! how long?" Martin continued, "but at last she has whispered to me, and I will go. Not as Bill Pete, no, but as the Mysterious Martin. I will go to the land of death and learn the everlasting secret, that has burnt my brain for twenty awful years.

"In the howling of the wind you will hear my scornful laughter, in the fury of the storm you will feel my anger, and be afraid."

All this time his eyes had been fixed on mine, and his face so close to me that I could feel his hot breath on my cheek, but now he straightened to his full height, and his hand stole behind him. When it reappeared, it was tightly clenched on the handle of a long hunting knife, that gleamed in the feeble lamplight.

"Tell me," he said, "will you go, too?" and he bent over me once more as a mother might stoop to caress her sleeping child. "Paul has trod that path, and Browne laughed as I struck him down, so surely you will not stay behind?"

Then, for the first time, in all that terrible night I found my voice:

"Help! help!" I shouted. "Murder!" and then I stopped to listen, but the wind, the everlasting wind, was my only answer.

"You were ever a weakling, Smithers," said the madman, and then, still bending over me, he slashed the knife through the arteries in his left wrist, so that the blood fell in a warm stream on my upturned face. At this new horror my senses left me.

When I opened my eyes again, the man still lived, although his blood was dry upon my cheek. He sat upon a stool before my bunk, his face white and drawn, but his eyes still shining brightly, while there came to my ears a steady, monotonous drip, drip, drip, like the summer rain on the roof at night.

Gradually, as I watched him, he sank lower and lower in his seat, till his chin rested on his breast, and yet how long, how very long, he took to die. The light seemed to be dying with him, slowly and surely, while the shadows in the corners, growing bolder now, crept out to watch the doomed man.

It may have been my imagination, but I could have sworn that I saw black shapes gliding through the semi-gloom, and once I distinctly heard a low laugh as though one were merry in the very chamber of death, and would hide it from the world.

The thunder had died away by now, but the storm still raged without, till it sounded like a horde of demons, waiting to seize Martin's wicked soul.

Suddenly there came a change in that grim figure that sat so silently. It moved, it shook itself, and rising to its full height, with arms thrown upward, seemed to grasp at the stars, while, strange to tell, the flame of the lamp, which had been burning low, now rose with it, till the whole room was bathed in a great white light.

"Oh, God!" cried the dying man. "Oh, God, Browne wins," and he fell face downward on the floor, a corpse.

Then there came a gust of wind that tore the blanket from the doorway, and that plunged the world into blackness.

....

Stuart found me, still tied to my bunk and raving in a high fever, while on the floor, with outstretched arms, lay the stiffening remains of the once Mysterious Martin.

The End

For Art's Sake

I

Burgess Martin! That was a name to conjure within literary circles a score of years ago. But how many are there now to whom it means more than an echo fast receding in the somber caverns of time? Not many, surely. And yet there was a period in New York's police annals when he juggled the sphere of art before the amazed eyes of the world, playing on the emotions of his readers with the deft touch of a master, instilling in our minds the strange, crimson thoughts which blossomed so abundantly on the twisted branch of his philosophy. And stepping back from life, calm and smiling, a famous toreador, he waved the red flag before the aroused, infuriated beast and waited. Those horns should gore sensitive humanity as a tribute to genius; while art, like a Nero, peered down from the balcony.

And the man's works—those two thin little volumes bound in red morocco, those two deadly little volumes which formerly crouched between the kindlier books in my library like crime-besmirched dwarfs—have they vanished

entirely from the memory of man? Vivid, poisonous
growths of mental fungi, those tales sprang to life only
to die before the sun. Quite perfect they were, and quite
malign. Handbooks of assassins, they——. But I must begin
at the beginning.

My younger brother, Paul, was responsible for bringing
Martin and me together. He had picked him up in some
Bohemian restaurant which he frequented and from that
time forward was so loud in his praises that natural curiosity
prompted me to see this paragon for myself.

"You must meet Burgess Martin, Charley," Paul said
one evening. "He's just the sort of chap you'd want to room
with in Paris. He's an artist to the core."

But I was not inclined to take my brother's statements
without a pinch of salt. My four years experience in college
ways—I was then a senior at Columbia University—had
made me slightly intolerant of freshman enthusiasm.
Besides Paul had already shown a marked tendency toward
strong drink and the false friendships that went with
it. On more than one occasion he had brought back to
our apartment "a good fellow" who needed considerable
moral persuasion to depart in the morning without a few
valuables. I have even known Paul's bibulous friends to
pocket saltcellars and spoons, so it is no wonder that his
laudatory statements about Martin at first did not move me.

"But I tell you he's an artist," Paul repeated
belligerently.

"What kind of an artist? Does he mix drinks
artistically?"

"Don't be a damn fool, Charley. Burgess Martin is the
most intelligent chap I ever met. He's in my class in English

literature and he knows more about the subject than Professor Brent himself."

"So you have discovered a genius in the freshman class," I said with all the weary tolerance of a senior. "What a strange anomaly! This year I thought they seemed especially unripened."

"Martin isn't. He makes what he says alive, somehow. You must really meet him, Charley. I'm going over to his rooms to-night. Why don't you come along?"

"You say he's going to Paris next fall to take up painting?"

"Yes, he'll study under Verone. If you two fellows hit it off, you might room together. Get your hat, Charley."

I could see that Paul had set his heart on my meeting his new friend and so I could no longer resist. "Now I'm in for a boring evening," I thought as I followed my brother out of the apartment.

Burgess Martin at that time lived in one of those dilapidated old boarding houses still to be found in the down-town section of New York City. This particular building seemed to be tottering on its foundation. It had a sodden, dissipated air about it—the air, in fact, of a *femme de monde* who realizes that she is aging. Here was the tomb of dead intrigue, of soiled romance.

We were admitted by a slatternly landlady and mounted two flights of rickety stairs. On the second landing Paul came to a halt and thundered on a door which was peeling like the face of a florid man who has sat too long in the sun. Almost immediately it swung open and I confronted that strange individual whose personality was one day to overshadow both our lives.

Burgess Martin was a tall man, well over six feet. He had one of those faces which seem to challenge time—a face that when young, looks old; and when old, seems young. It was long, lean, ascetic—the lips, colorless and thin; the nose, hooked and warlike; the eyes, small and grey with the piercing quality of gimlets; the forehead, a threatening protuberance which overshadowed the rest and hinted at phenomenal intellectual powers. His body was thin, almost to the point of emaciation; yet, for all that, one sensed a great virility stirring in that skeleton frame.

I was immediately conscious of this virility and of something which perhaps sprang from it. The man exuded an unpleasant atmosphere, an atmosphere very difficult to resist; His personality, like an octopus, wound its many cold arms of reason about one. To struggle against it was useless and yet one struggled automatically. Genius is one of the most irritating traits in others. To acknowledge it, one must bend the stiff neck of self-pride.

Perhaps my nerves were a trifle out of tune at the time. It is the only way I have of accounting for that strange sensation which ran through me as Martin's thin, cool hand slipped into mine. I felt as though I had a precious secret which must be guarded at all costs and which even now was threatened. The man's unfeeling grey eyes were fixed intently on me; those eyes which, like magnets, seemed to be drawing my ego out of my body.

"Have a seat, gentlemen. And help yourselves to those cigarettes."

Martin turned to Paul and I felt instant relief. Seating myself in one of the rickety chairs the room afforded, I lit a cigarette and passed the box to my host.

"No, thank you," he said a trifle bruskly. "I don't smoke. It wastes too much time."

"Are you so busy as all that?" I asked. "I had no idea the freshman requirements were especially stiff. In my time, one could squeeze through without much work."

Martin's thin lips drew up at the corners like a cat's. It was his nearest approach to a smile. "My dear fellow," said he, "I hadn't my college work in mind. Of course, that's childishly simple. I am trying to perfect myself in one or two of the arts and that requires time when one hasn't the proper guidance."

"The proper guidance!" I murmured. "Surely Professor Brent is a competent teacher of English literature. He's had several books of essays published."

Again Martin's lips drew up at the corners. "A small man," said he "—a small man with a small mind. His work fairly bristles with penny-whistle platitudes. All his sunny little essays are woven out of the worsted mottoes our grandmothers used to frame and hang on the wall: 'Be good and you'll be happy,' 'Virtue is its own reward,' 'If at first you don't succeed, why try, try again.' What sickening, sentimental slop! Teach *me* literature? Why, he can't even teach himself!"

Martin's words and the sneering contempt with which they were uttered, made me boil inwardly. My college career had formed me into the usual type of undergraduate to whom the institutions of the university were sacred matters not lightly to be tampered with. Professor Brent had grown grey in service and had even made his voice heard in the outer world; yet here was a green freshman attempting to overthrow him! What consummate conceit! But I would put this young ass in his place.

"Perhaps you can tell me how Professor Brent's essay on man could be improved upon," I said coldly. "I happen to have the book with me."

"Oh, I say, Charley," Paul broke in, running his hand through his hair, "that's his very best essay! Of course, there's nothing much wrong with it."

But Martin's grey eyes brightened as he took the small leather volume I offered him. "Without doubt the ideas expressed in it are puerile," said he, opening the book to the essay in question. "Let us examine the style. Ah, just as I thought—stiff, laborious—a very poor flow of words."

"Could *you* do as well?" I asked ironically. The man's insufferable egotism grated on my nerves like sandpaper.

"Much better," he answered simply. "Come, I'll prove it. You are familiar with this essay, I presume?"

"I know it by heart."

"So much the better. Now I'll read it as it should have been written, transposing as I go along."

Martin bent his brows over the essay while my brother and I interchanged glances. Although I tapped my forehead with a meaning forefinger, Paul smiled triumphantly. Evidently he had perfect confidence in his new-found acquaintance.

Now our host's voice broke the silence—a voice, rich, vibrant, which carried one along with it as on a swiftly moving stream. And, strange to say, although the meaning of the essay was in no manner changed, the style was entirely altered. New life seemed to have been infused into every line. The sentences glowed with poetic fire. My artistic sense was stirred by such a perfect phraseology. It seemed well nigh impossible that any man could read on without hesitation and transpose so remarkably.

"Splendid!" I cried when he had done. "But surely you worked that out before?"

"I never even read it until just now," he answered, smiling at Paul. "Really, I wouldn't waste my time over such material. Well, did I improve upon it?"

"That's a matter of opinion," I muttered, overcoming my admiration with a mighty effort. "Personally, I've always liked Brent's style."

"Own up when you're beaten, Charley," Paul cried. "There's no comparison. I'm a dub about most highbrow matters, but even *I* realize that Martin has improved it."

"That's a matter of opinion," I repeated stubbornly.

Martin raised his eyebrows and regarded me quizzically. "You don't appear to have much literary taste," said he. "However, that won't hold you back as a painter. Paul tells me that you intend studying under Verone. Perhaps we can hire a studio together." He rose to his feet. "I've a painting in my bedroom which might interest you."

"Yes, indeed, I would like to see it."

Martin strode into an adjoining room and returned almost immediately with a canvas under his arm. Placing it in a position where the light touched it effectively, he stepped back.

"There you have it," said he.

I uttered an exclamation of surprise at what I saw. To my as yet untrained eye, it seemed a truly remarkable piece of work. And it affected me strangely. Although it was very warm in the room, I felt a wave of intense cold pass through my frame, followed almost immediately by a sensation of acute nausea.

The painting which affected me thus was startling in its conception. It depicted a young girl lying dead on a country road blocked with snow. Desolate and forsaken, she lay there, her white face upturned to the leaden sky. Blood was streaming from her neck and slowly sinking into the snow. And all about her the tiny flakes were still falling—a thick veil of them which shut in this tragedy completely from the outer world. Somewhere in the swirling background, a dark shape lurked—an evil, twisted shape, vague and unreal as a distant dream. Was it the assassin, or was it merely the shadow of approaching night? As I watched, it seemed to stir slightly.

"Why, this is the work of a great artist!" I cried in amazement. "Did *you* paint it?"

"Yes," he answered slowly. "But it won't do. It's very crude."

"Crude! Why, it fairly stands out of the canvas. I think it's a masterpiece; you're too modest."

"That's what *I* say," Paul chimed in. "He's entirely too modest."

"I'm nothing of the sort," Martin said contemptuously. "No one is actually modest and only fools pretend to be."

"But where did you get the idea?" I asked. "It's a remarkable conception."

"The girl was a friend of mine. One afternoon I found her lying dead in the road with her throat sliced from ear to ear. Of course, I was thoroughly shocked; but I realized perfectly what an excellent model she made. I couldn't resist making a sketch of her just as she was."

"Who murdered her?" I asked.

"No one knows."

"And you mean to say, Burgess, that you made a sketch of her while she lay bleeding there!" Paul cried.

"Don't tell me that you're such a hard-hearted brute as all that! I don't believe a word of it."

Martin regarded him for a moment with a kind of cold curiosity in his grey eyes. "I see that you read me like an open book, Paul," he murmured.

"Not at all. But no one could sit down calmly beside a murdered friend and make a sketch of her. The thing is impossible."

"Perhaps. But that is exactly how she looked when I found her."

"What was the motive for the crime?" I asked.

"Apparently no motive," Martin answered with a shrug of his shoulders. "Or, at least, none that could be discovered. But let's say no more about it. It's a nasty story and brings back unpleasant recollections."

Soon the talk drifted into other channels. Martin gave us a glimpse into his childhood which must have been far from a happy one. At an early age he had lost both parents and had been adopted by an eccentric aunt who had taken him to live with her in a lonely house far out in the country. This aunt had had many peculiarities. A firm believer in spiritualism, considering herself a medium, she had often taken her small nephew into a dark room at the top of the house where she carried on ghostly conversations with the dead.

"I was only six years old at the time," Martin finished, "and you can readily understand what effect such treatment had on my forming mind."

"What became of her?" I asked.

"She died at last and went to join her spirit friends. But long before that I knew the whole thing to be a farce.

She left me ten thousand a year which is some recompense for all she made me suffer."

At that time ten thousand a year seemed to me a princely income. I would willingly have put up with a dozen eccentric aunts to have secured it. Something of this must have been written on my face, for Martin's lips once more curled up at the corners into a grimace which was half smile and half sneer.

"Yes, ten thousand a year," he repeated slowly. "Much more than I spend, for I believe that an artist should live without the luxuries of life. I tell you all this, of course, because I would like to have you with me in Paris and don't think you would readily room with a pauper."

"After seeing your work, I would room with you if you hadn't a cent," I said warmly. "The thing is settled as far as I am concerned."

II

During the remainder of the college year Paul saw
Burgess Martin daily. A close friendship sprang up between
the two which was to me, at least, unaccountable. They
were such direct opposites that such an alliance seemed
altogether beyond the bounds of reason. Perhaps, after all,
real warmth is obtained only by rubbing together two quite
dissimilar substances.

Paul had been going down hill steadily ever since
entering college the previous fall. He was one of those
unfortunate men over whom alcohol in any form has a
deadly influence. High spirited, generous to a fault, full
of the joy of life, my younger brother was a delightful
companion and one of the most popular freshmen in the
university. But let him have a few drinks and soon a startling
transformation would take place. He would become
morose, intolerant, prone to fly into a rage at the slightest
provocation. Then would follow a period of deep depression

which bordered on melancholia—a dangerous mental state when I have known him to contemplate suicide.

But Martin, in some miraculous fashion, succeeded in curing him. Paul no longer returned at night the worse for liquor. He gave up café life altogether and took up reading seriously. I often saw him in the college library browsing over some book which Martin had recommended. In those last few weeks of the spring term, he succeeded in passing his examinations.

The following autumn found Martin and me snugly ensconced in a comfortable apartment in Paris. My father provided me with an ample income to pursue my artistic studies and I was not slow in spending it and making acquaintances in the Latin Quarter.

Those were happy days. Our studio soon became the meeting-place of congenial spirits. Martin struck the one jarring note in an otherwise perfect harmony. Among those gay chattering magpies of art, he seemed as somber and solitary as a crow. He avoided my guests as much as possible; behind his back, they called him "Monsieur la Nuit." He had an especial detestation of women, alluding to them very much as a man might speak of some deadly and prevalent disease. When he heard the swish of their skirts on our landing, he would lock himself in his bed-room and not come out again until they had gone. "A true artist can have but one mistress—his art," he was wont to say. "The rest are leeches."

Although I failed to share my roommate's views, I never allowed friends to interfere with my work. I improved rapidly. Often our instructor, the famous Verone, stood before my easel longer than was his wont with the other students. Martin's drawings alone overshadowed mine; yet I felt vaguely that they were disappointing to the master.

One bright sunshiny afternoon in May, Emile Verone rested his hand for a moment on my shoulder. "Ah, monsieur," he murmured, "you have talent and your heart is in it. There is life in that figure. You have caught it in a web of youth. Bravo!"

Leaving me jubilant, he passed on to Martin's easel. Here he remained motionless for several moments, a frown of perplexity creasing his forehead, gazing at my roommate's canvas in the manner of a man attempting to read a riddle.

"It is good—very good," I heard him mutter. "And yet there is something lacking. It is not technique, it is feeling. It——. Ah, I have guessed your little secret. Your heart is not in your task. Am I not right, Monsieur Martin?"

"Perfectly," Martin answered, glancing up. "The model is not to my taste. That big, fat peasant with a face like a pumpkin does not inspire me."

I knew of Verone's hasty temper and was prepared for some manifestation of it. My roommate's answer had been rather unceremonious. But the little Frenchman did not appear to be the least bit ruffled. His voice suddenly sank into a soothing murmur.

"Quite so," he said mildly. "Every artist has his likes and his dislikes. But I have a plan. Absent yourself from the class for a month and choose a model for yourself. I will be anxiously awaiting the result. Does that satisfy you, monsieur?"

"Yes, indeed," Martin answered with a strange glint in his grey eyes. "Nothing could suit me better."

During the days that followed I saw very little of my roommate. He would leave the studio each morning, his portfolio under his arm, and not return again till the shadows of nightfall. And the few hours which he did spend in the apartment were spent in the privacy of his bedroom behind a locked door.

To tell the truth, I was relieved by his absence. The man was like a wet blanket thrown on the bonfire of good-fellowship which I was attempting to kindle in the studio. My guests were ill at ease in his company; and I, myself, felt a strange irritation at his every word and gesture. Now, as I look back on it, I think it was his atmosphere—that ever-present atmosphere of personal power—which we could not forgive him and which was as gall and wormwood to our own growing personalities.

One night, while champagne corks were popping merrily and laughter echoed through the studio, Martin's bedroom door swung open and he stepped into our midst. His face was a deathly white and there were great, black hollows under his eyes. Instantly our laughter died away.

"Pour yourself a glass of wine," I said with forced heartiness. "Have you come to join the merry-makers?"

"Just that," Martin muttered.

"What have you been doing with yourself?" one of my guests asked. "You're as pale as a ghost, monsieur."

"I've been living with a corpse for a month," Martin said slowly. "Would you like to see the results?"

He turned and re-entered his bedroom. A moment later he glided out again with a canvas under his arm. Placing it on the mantelpiece where we could all get a good view of it, he turned toward us and said in his deep, sonorous voice: "Allow me to introduce to you the results, gentlemen."

Again there was silence, broken only by the deep breathing of those about me. All eyes were fixed on the painting. For many moments we stared at it, spellbound, motionless. It was the most sincere tribute I have seen paid to a living artist. There were two or three men present that night who afterward became international figures; but, at the moment, we knew in our souls that there was but one great master and that he now stood before us.

What was there in this painting to move us so? It is beyond my feeble pen to describe adequately the sensations of horror with which it filled me,—horror, overmastering and vaguely sinister; horror whose breath was cold and damp as the tomb. One seemed to enter that picture bodily; to enter it and lose oneself in the shadows.

The painting represented the morgue in the dim twilight and more especially the body of a man lying on one of the marble slabs. The upturned face of the corpse was a mottled green shade; the protruding eyes were covered with a kind of fungus. And to add to its horror, the bristling chin had dropped, disclosing two yellow fangs in a ghastly grin. On either side of this grim figure, partly revealed in the semi-gloom, were other slabs—each the bed of some new fantastic terror. Underneath this revolting conception was written in English these four words, "He Laughs at Death."

We toasted Martin with brimming glasses, we shook him by the hand, we called him "master." And he, for once, shook off his cloak of aloofness. Indeed, he put himself out to amuse us, telling us stories so intensely droll that we roared with laughter till all unconsciously our eyes returned to the painting. Then, as the laughter died in our throats, as the smiles faded from our faces, I thought I saw his lips curl in triumph.

III

Emile Verone went into ecstasies over Martin's painting, calling it "a masterpiece of the terrible"; and soon it became noised abroad that my roommate was one of those rare freaks of nature, a genius. Art students now began to seek Martin out as a profitable acquaintance. But he refused to be drawn out of his cocoon of solitude and mystery. His personality, as always, enwrapped him like an impenetrable coat of mail. Would-be friends and admirers flinched when they met his cold grey eyes. Soon the first fine edge of their excitement wore off; they gave him up as impossible with a shrug of the shoulders and a muttered "Monsieur la Nuit."

Time passed quickly. Almost before I realized it, a year rolled by. Martin had worked diligently; now the walls of our studio were covered with morbid masterpieces. As one might imagine, a highly strung person could not have entered this apartment for the first time without an inward

tremor. Indeed, when the lights burned low, the room
seemed to be a veritable charnel-house.

One gloomy afternoon in autumn, these paintings
were too much for my self-control. I was on the brink of
a serious sickness at the time; and, as I sat alone before
the dying fire, the flickering flames would reveal first one
stiffening horror and then another till my overtaxed nerves
could stand no more. Leaping to my feet with a muttered
curse, I began turning those ghastly painted faces to the
wall.

Suddenly I heard a low laugh behind me. Wheeling
about, I encountered Martin who had entered as noiselessly
as a cat. His sallow face still wore a crooked, evil smile
which creased his right cheek like a scar.

"Emile Verone is right," he said, moistening his lips
with his tongue. "No one will buy my paintings because
they are too good, too realistic in their horror. And if they
were sold by any chance, they would be banished to the
attic. Who would live with the dead but Martin?"

Suddenly I felt sick—deathly sick. I had the strange
sensation of having some precious secret drawn from me
against my will—the same sensation, in fact, that I had
experienced once before. Then followed dizziness and
helplessness. Martin's face appeared to loom above me,
gigantic, monstrous. It grew larger and larger—a huge,
terrifying mask behind which an evil passion lurked.
Suppose he should remove this mask? Ah, it was slipping
now, slipping—

Everything grew black before my eyes. I felt a sharp
blow on my forehead, then numbness and nothingness. I
had fallen over in a swoon.

For the duration of that week I was delirious with typhoid fever. Strange dreams tormented me, and in these dreams Martin was always the central figure. I can still remember one of them distinctly.

I felt that I was lying naked on the scorching sands of a desert beneath the rays of a blistering sun. It was useless to struggle; I was held down by some invisible weight. And over my bare, burning body an army of tiny ants was crawling, causing me acute agony. But just as my sufferings were at their height, Martin's lean face bent over me, his cold grey eyes peered curiously into mine, and he said earnestly: "How do you feel now?"

When I at last came out of the land of delirium, I was as weak as a new-born child. The sun was streaming through the window, casting its javelins of light on every side. One of them lay across the bed like a bar of molten gold. It occurred to me that I would like to feel its reassuring warmth, but I had scarcely enough strength to reach out my hand.

Suddenly Martin's voice broke the silence. "How do you feel now?" he asked.

I started at these words which had echoed through my dreams. I had to steady myself before I answered feebly: "Much better, thank you."

During the next few days I improved rapidly. Martin was a competent nurse. Sitting beside my bed, he whiled away the tedious hours by his remarkable knack of story-telling. It was not the stories themselves which held me—he would often repeat those I had already heard—but his truly remarkable wording which made them flow as smoothly as a river of oil and was as pleasing to the ear as music.

Sometimes I would speak of Paul, and then Martin would be the eager listener. I received several letters from home. One of these worried me. It was from my father and ran as follows:

Dear Charles: Paul is drinking again. I can do nothing with him. The slightest reprimand drives him into a frenzy of remorse and despondency. At such times he is quite capable of taking his own life. I wish you were home. Perhaps you could manage him.

Affectionately, Dad.

This letter came while I was still very weak and I asked Martin to read it aloud to me. I saw his face darken as he perused it. When he had finished, he sat in gloomy silence. At last I heard him mutter: "It's in his blood. I could handle him, but another might take the wrong way. It would be fatal to—"

"You must think a great deal of Paul," I broke in.

"A great deal?" he cried vehemently. "Why, Paul means more to me than my art! Do you think I would have wasted my time pulling *you* out of the valley of death if you weren't his brother?"

He rose without waiting to hear my response and hurried from the room. Although it may seem surprising, I was relieved by what he had just said. I had never liked the fellow; and to be weighed down under a load of obligations to one heartily disliked, is a very unpleasant experience. If he had nursed me back to health merely on account of his friendship for Paul, surely I did not owe him as much as if he had been actuated solely out of regard for me.

Soon I was strong enough to leave my bed and sit up for an hour or so each day. For three weeks I had been living on a diet of milk and broth, but now the doctor allowed me solid foods. Ah, the joy of eating when one is recovering from typhoid! It repays one for all those earlier sufferings.

One evening as I was waiting impatiently for supper to be served, I heard Martin's bedroom door open. A moment later he entered, carrying a suitcase. A mutual coldness had sprung up between us, but this unusual sight made me forget everything.

"Why, where are you going?" I cried in astonishment.

"Home," he answered, placing the suitcase on the floor.

"Not to America, surely?"

"Where else?"

"But your art? How about your painting?"

"Oh, I'm giving that up," he said in a matter-of-fact voice.

"Giving it up!" I cried. "After what you've already done! Why, you will be recognized by the world in another year or so! You must be mad!"

"Do you think so?"

"I know so!" I answered with some heat. "What else could you turn your hand to with the same success? Art, such as yours, springs from the soul. By renouncing it, you would be tearing out the best in you."

"I will have to do that in any case to follow the career which I have planned for myself."

"What is this precious career?"

"Literature," he answered calmly. "I took up drawing merely to illustrate my stories. No other man could do them justice."

"So you are one of those numerous young men who think they can write," I said in a tone which brought a flush to his sallow cheeks. "What reason have you to suppose so?"

"You must acknowledge that I can tell a story."

"Yes, but your stories are not original. Have you a keen imagination?"

"Not a vestige of one," he said simply.

"Then how can you expect to become a successful writer? A literary man without any imagination is doomed to failure from the start."

"You are wrong—entirely wrong!"

"How so?" I demanded.

"Because a writer does not necessarily need a creative imagination," he said a trifle wearily. "I, myself, have what is far better—a concise memory and the ability to write in the most perfect wording exactly what I see and feel. There is enough going on in the world at this moment to serve as the substance for a million stories. Of course, one has to branch away from the beaten path to find such material. But that is exactly what I am going to do."

"But you haven't mingled enough with other men," I hastened to add. "You know little or nothing of human nature. A man to be a successful writer"—I was quoting Professor Brent—"must be a student and admirer of his fellow men. Without companionship, a writer misses the human touch."

Martin's lips curled up at the corners in one of his irritating smiles. "My dear Smithers," he said in a tone which he might have used in speaking to a tiresome child, "you're entirely at fault in such a surmise. Surely an onlooker, a mere spectator with no party feeling of any kind, can witness the battle of life with better results than can the actual combatants. You say that a writer should study and admire his fellowmen. That is impossible. If we admire a man, we cannot study him. We are prematurely blinded to all but his virtues. By taking that attitude toward mankind at large, we lose the larger half of faults and follies which go into the makeup of the average mortal."

"I don't agree with you," I said coldly. "But even if you were right, you'd be a fool to throw away a certainty for an obscure possibility. Have you stopped to think that the successful writer of to-day has to cater to the mob as you call them?"

"But *I* won't have to do that," he cried with flashing eyes. "I intend devoting my time exclusively to horror tales. Have you ever witnessed an accident on the street? Well, in a moment, hundreds collect where there was but one. They are drawn thither by that morbid streak in humanity, that overmastering desire to feast one's eyes on gruesome details. Such a sensation will be gratified in my stories. Men and women will buy them to experience the delightful tremor of tragedy beside their own firesides. Who would not walk many blocks to see a murder committed? Nearly all of us would go if our own precious lives were not endangered. I tell you the public will snatch up my work because it will give them the exact sensation of those who stand about on tiptoe to catch a glimpse of death."

In spite of myself, his words stirred my imagination. Was it possible that literature could be made as vivid as this? He had succeeded in portraying horror most realistically with the pigments of the painter, but could he create such an atmosphere with cold words alone? No, it was impossible—even laughably absurd.

"You cannot possibly create such an acute feeling in the minds of your readers," I said at length. "No man could do it."

"What no man can do, *I* can do," Martin replied with insufferable egotism. "I will surely succeed as a writer—as surely as you will fail as a painter."

"Really!" I cried with a sneer. "Emile Verone thinks rather highly of my work."

"Your work is promising now because you paint as your eye tells you. But later, when you get out into the world, it will be different."

"In what way?" I asked.

"Because a successful portrait painter—bear in mind that I am speaking from the commercial, worldly standpoint when I say successful—must be nothing more or less than a beauty doctor. Men and women do not wish to be painted as they are, but as they *think* they are. Flatter them cleverly enough, and you'll soon become what the world considers a successful artist. What a soul-stirring vocation! Your watchword through life shall be: "When I touch my patron's vanity I also touch his pocketbook.""

"I'll never do that—not if I have to starve first!" I cried angrily.

But Martin only smiled unpleasantly and picked up his suitcase. With a curt nod, he turned and strode out of the room. A moment late I heard the outer door slam. He had gone.

IV

That same week Martin sailed for home. He left behind him his gruesome paintings which he bequeathed to me in a sarcastic note. I immediately removed those grisly masterpieces and hung up in their place some of my own work. At the time I was living a trifle beyond my means; and so, when I received what I then considered a handsome offer from Emile Verone for my roommate's morbid creations, I was glad enough to accept it. Of course I intended paying Martin the price I received for them at some future date—a date which, unfortunately, never materialized. These same paintings, I now understand, hang in the Louvre and are worth their weight in gold.

After Martin had left Paris, I began to look around for another roommate who would share my expenses. One evening, as luck would have it, I happened to run into an old acquaintance at the Follies Bergere. He had wandered to Paris alone to amuse himself and was delighted at the prospect of living with a former college friend who knew the ropes.

Wilbur Huntington was a plump young man who had made quite a reputation for himself at the university. No one had ever caught him in the act of opening a book, yet he had always glided smoothly through the examinations. He was an anomaly to the professors who claimed that success required effort. His half-shut, sleepy, brown eyes, his bland smile, his round, expressionless face, quite belied the man's intelligence. Although he was lazy to a fault, his mind was as keen as a knife which had just visited the grindstone. I have never met his equal as a psychologist.

I was lucky to have fallen in with him. He came of a very wealthy New York family, who gave him a lavish income—an income which he was not slow in spending. Money meant little or nothing to him. During the months we roomed together we lived like fighting cocks.

There was nothing Huntington liked better than to fill our studio with Emile Verone's pupils and discuss art. He would start the ball rolling with some titbit of knowledge which he had picked up; start it rolling, and then sink back comfortably on the lounge, close his narrow-lidded eyes and smile blandly at the ceiling. He liked to hear the maniacs rave, as he expressed it. In the Latin Quarter he was called "Le Cochon d'Inde." They facetiously brought him offerings of lettuce leaves which he devoured solemnly and rapaciously. The man's appetite was amazing.

With such a companion, the months sped by merrily. Occasionally I received a letter from home. It seemed that Paul had reformed, and that this reformation had been brought about through Martin. Apparently my former roommate had sought him out immediately on his return to America and had once more succeeded where others had failed. The letter, which informed me of this, was written by my mother. It ran as follows:

My Dear Son: You will be glad to know that Paul has given up drinking. What a relief this has been to your father and me! We have been so worried about him since you left home! But now everything seems to be all right.

We owe Paul's reformation to your friend, Mr. Martin. He has a remarkable influence over the boy. And yet, somehow, I can't bring myself to like him. When he is in the room, I always feel as though I had a precious secret which I must keep from him at all cost. This is absurd, of course.

My dear boy, I am glad that you are getting along so well in your studies! I hope you will come home soon. Father has not been in good health lately. I believe he has been worrying over business affairs.

Lovingly, Mother.

At the time I did not give much heed to the last few lines of my mother's letter. Father had always been such a strong, robust man that I could not imagine him sick. Death and failure seemed quite remote from him. And so, when I received a letter from Paul two months later, I was quite unprepared for what it had to tell me. The news which it contained was like a bolt from the blue. I quote it here:

Dear Charley: Come home at once. Father died this morning, and we need you. Only yesterday

I learned that the firm had failed. Would write
more, but mother is calling. Hurry home.

Affectionately, Paul.

"What's the trouble?" Huntington asked. He had come
into the studio unnoticed and now stood at my elbow.
"What's the trouble?" he repeated. "You're as white as a
ghost."

I tried to answer him but couldn't. Something clicked
in my throat like a clock running down. I handed him the
letter in silence.

"I don't know what to say," he muttered a moment
later. "I'm awfully sorry, Charley. I want you to know that."
He offered me his plump hand boyishly.

But I did not see it. There were weak, womanly tears
in my eyes. Father was dead—not only dead but ruined!
I had pictured to myself two more years in Paris and then
a luxurious studio in New York; and now these air castles
had crumbled in an instant. But what a selfish brute I was!
Father had just died, and I was already thinking of myself.
Martin had been right in his estimate of me.

"*The Marseillaise* sails to-morrow," Huntington said.
"I'll hustle down and get our staterooms reserved."

"But surely you're not going to leave Paris?" I
murmured. "I can make it all right by myself."

Huntington smiled sleepily. "Don't you worry about
that," he answered. "I'm sick of Paris. When *you* go, *I* go.
Besides, as you know, queer birds are my hobby; and I'm
rather anxious to meet this chap, Martin, of whom you have
told me so much."

On the following day we took passage for New York.
The ocean was rather rough for that time of year; to my

natural depression were added the qualms of seasickness. But on that trip I learned the true worth of the plump, sleepy man whom my associates of the Latin Quarter called "Le Cochon d'Inde." He was indefatigable in his efforts to cheer me up.

I found affairs at home even worse than I had imagined. My father had died a bankrupt. He had left nothing except the house which was heavily mortgaged and several debts incurred during his illness. These bills, added to the natural grief attending his death, had aged my mother at least ten years. I had, indeed, come home at the right moment if I could help.

My one pleasant surprise was Paul. He had matured considerably in the last few years. I found him looking splendidly—a handsome, capable fellow, if there ever was one. On the first night of my homecoming we had a long talk together after mother had gone to bed.

"They tell me you're not drinking any more, Paul?" I said casually.

"No," he answered with a grim smile. "I'm through with that stuff for good. Martin cured me."

"How did he go about it?" I asked.

"Oh, he showed me a few examples of what it could do to a fellow. You see he's living in the slums these days, and he has lots of opportunity to study drunks in their last stages."

"In the slums? Why does he live there?"

"He's gathering material for a book on murder—studying the criminal types close up. He says it pays to get first-hand knowledge of a subject. When I begin practicing law, he'll send me a lot of clients."

"When do you go up for your final examinations?"
"Next month—thanks to Martin. If it weren't for him,
I'd probably be hitting the high life yet. But one night
he collared me, dragged me over to his tenement, and
introduced me to a bleary-eyed old chap who was fighting
imaginary snakes. What a sight he was!" Paul passed his
hands across his eyes as though to shut out a picture. "He
had been a gentleman, too, in his day—a Harvard man, I
believe. Any one could tell he wasn't an ordinary drunk by
his ravings. He quoted a lot of poetry to keep off the snakes.
Dante's Inferno I believe it was. Well, it cured me."

"I'm glad of that. But you mustn't give Martin all the
credit. A great deal belongs to you."

"Not a bit," he answered with a rueful shake of his
head. "Martin scared me into it. But what are you going do
now, Charley? Are you going to paint portraits?"

"Yes, if I can get any sitters. I've got to look around a
bit first. You don't know any wealthy beauty who wants to
have her face immortalized?"

Paul rose yawning. "No," he answered. "But if I did, I
don't think I'd hand her over to you until I had discovered
if there weren't some legitimate, legal way of separating her
from her cash."

The next day I began writing letters to former
acquaintances with the hope that they might know of some
one who was anxious to have a portrait painted by a pupil
of the famous Emile Verone. I soon learned that I could
hope for little from this source. Most of my college friends
were so busy or so absent-minded that they failed to answer
my note; and the few replies which I did receive were far
from encouraging. Evidently the world at large was not at

all interested in furthering the future of an aspiring young genius.

The pile of bills in my mother's desk grew higher day by day. I no longer dared to open them. My spirits were at very low ebb on the morning when I received a note from Wilbur Huntington which gave me a ray of hope. It ran as follows:

Dear Charley: The mater wants her portrait painted. She's not much on looks, but she has a well-lined pocketbook. I have boosted you to the skies. She now thinks that you are a Van Dyke, a Whistler, and a Sargent, all in one. Call on her next Monday and make good.

As ever, Wilbur.

When I finished this hope-inspiring epistle, I uttered a whoop of joy which brought Paul out on the veranda in no time. "I've struck it at last," I cried.

"What's the matter?" he asked. "Have you found a half-dollar or something?"

"I've found a good many half-dollars," I answered gleefully. "I've been asked to do a portrait of Mrs. Huntington—you know, Wilbur Huntington's mother. It's the chance of a lifetime. If I make good, she'll recommend me to her society friends and it will be smooth sailing after that."

"Good man!" cried Paul. "You've struck it all right. But look here. I've got another surprise for you."

"What is it?" I asked.

"It's a story by Martin," he answered. "They're featuring it this month in the Footstool magazine. Just look

it over while I run downtown. I want your opinion of it. It's
the first piece of work he's had published."

After Paul had gone, I opened the magazine. On the
first page was an illustration by Martin himself. I recognized
it instantly. It was a miniature of that first painting I had
seen of his—that vivid conception of the girl lying dead in
the snow. It had been improved by a few deft strokes of the
brush so that now it was a veritable masterpiece of mystery.
For a long moment I gazed at it while the well-remembered
feeling of intense cold passed through my frame. At last,
with an effort, I turned the page. "The Murder of Mary
Mortimer," was the title of the story.

"Some melodramatic nonsense, no doubt," I told
myself and began to read.

But from the first page I knew that I was wrong—
entirely wrong. I could not blind myself to the truth. If the
man's illustration was gruesome and yet masterful, the man's
story was diabolic and yet a classic.

As I read, I felt the same sensations stirring in me that
the deformed idiot in Martin's story felt when the voice
whispered in his ear: "You are losing her! Is it not better
to have her dead?" And when he is driven by this voice to
strike her down, when she falls like a red ruin in the snow,
I saw that scene as though I were standing where the dark
shadows of nightfall were closing in.

"I see you like my story," said a familiar voice.

I looked up with a start and encountered Martin's cold
grey eyes. His thin lips were curling up at the corners in
their wonted cat-like grimace. For a moment I experienced
the unpleasant nervous shock of a somnambulist who is
suddenly awakened.

"A remarkable story!" I said at length in a rather unsteady tone. "The most startlingly vivid piece of fiction I ever read! Surely you must have imagination to write like that?"

"On the contrary, not a grain of it. As I told you once before, there are countless themes drifting about and a man has only to get off the beaten path to find them. Without exaggeration I can say that I have done so."

"Your story proves that," I assented. "But where did you get the idea?"

Again his lips writhed into an unpleasant smile. "That would be revealing my little secret," he murmured, wagging his head reprovingly at me. "A wise angler never tells where he caught his last trout."

"Your story is founded on truth?" I asked.

"It would seem so. A man without imagination cannot lie artistically."

"But I don't believe that even a weak-minded person could be turned into a murderer by mental suggestion. It's preposterous! That's the weak spot in your story, Martin."

He threw back his head and burst into a laugh—if you could call a series of sounds so inhuman a laugh. It was as hoarse and guttural as the cawing of a crow. At last he broke off and regarded me solemnly.

"Smithers," he said, "you amuse me. In fact, you are the one man in the world who can make me laugh."

By this time I was thoroughly aroused. This man's colossal egotism was unendurable. "You may laugh as much as you please," I cried, "but that isn't answering my criticism of your story. I repeat that mental suggestion cannot form even a weak-minded person into a murderer. Your tale doesn't ring true to life."

"Perhaps so," he murmured. "I thought that it could be managed by mental suggestion—under the right circumstances, of course. But where is Paul this morning?"

"He went downtown," I said brusquely. "He probably won't be back for an hour or two."

"Well, I'll not wait. Tell him I called, won't you? Good-bye, Smithers."

For some time I sat watching his tall, lean figure receding in the distance. Finally I rose, and, moved by a sudden fit of childish irritation, picked up the magazine, entered the library, and deposited it carefully on a bed of glowing coals.

"It's better out of the way," I told myself. I never knew until years later how truly I had spoken.

V

It was not long before Martin's prophecy about my career came true. Spurred on by adversity and a natural desire to please I soon became one of those flourishing society portrait painters who fatten on the vanity of women. Mrs. Huntington's picture did not suit her until I had touched it up to such an extent that her own son could not recognize any likeness. But when I had beautified her to her heart's content, she became enthusiastic and recommended me to all her wealthy friends. That was the beginning. Soon I had all I could do to fill the many orders which rained down on me. My work became the vogue—I was no longer a man but a fashion.

Prosperity brought the fulfillment of my youthful dreams. I was now able to rent and fit out one of the most artistic studios in Washington Square. But, in spite of this, I was far from happy. I had moments of deep depression when my work galled me cruelly—moments when the only

spur that kept me going was the knowledge that before long
I could retire and live a life of leisure.

Meanwhile Paul had passed his examinations to the
bar and was actually practicing. No sooner had he hung
out his shingle than he was besieged daily by a ragged
multitude of clients whom he shrewdly suspected Martin
had sent his way. A stream of villainous faces passed through
his office at all hours—faces which one could imagine as
being associated with every crime in the calendar. Paul had
a keen mind; he soon developed into a criminal lawyer of
exceptional reputation. His clients, in spite of their poverty-
stricken appearance, paid him well for his services and he
soon became affluent.

I saw a great deal of my brother at this time. We had
become much closer friends. The four years which divided
us no longer seemed such an insurmountable barrier. Now
he would often take me into his confidence.

There was only one topic on which we could not agree.
Paul was still an ardent admirer of Martin; while I, although
I had to acknowledge the man's gifts, loathed the very
mention of his name. I could not forgive him his prophecy
concerning my career. Yes, that afternoon in Paris, he had
told me what I would soon become. And because he had
seen so clearly into the hidden recesses of my character, I
felt that I would hate him till the end. It is primitive but
human to resist the prying eyes of genius. The ego—that
most precious possession of man—is outraged to find itself
held up before the clear, steady flame of psychological
insight.

Paul had a way of referring to Martin which was
extremely annoying to me. He would repeat over and over
again that he owed everything to him. It used to make me

very angry to hear him belittle his own success by such a quixotic statement. Surely he owed a large measure of his practice to his own acuteness and perseverance. Often we would argue about it.

"Yes," Paul would say, glancing about his well-appointed library, "I owe all this to him. He cured me of drunkenness and sent me my clients."

"Nonsense! Perhaps he *did* help to cure you and perhaps he sent you a few clients; but if you hadn't had strength of will enough to leave the liquor alone and strength of mind enough to win the majority of your cases, his help wouldn't have amounted to much."

But Paul would shake his head obstinately and repeat: "He has done everything for me—everything."

And then I would generally lose my temper and express my true feelings. "How about that book he is writing? He may be able to make *you*, but he doesn't seem to be able to make himself. He's been writing for over two years now and has had only one story in print. Won't the publishers take his work?"

Now Paul, in his turn, would flush angrily and his blue eyes would grow darker. "How should I know? He never talks about himself. But I'll tell you this, Charley—when his work *is* published, the whole world will know about it!"

Often, after one of these heated controversies, I would leave my brother's apartment in a temper and walk the streets for hours before I regained my habitual calm. It was on one of these midnight rambles that I met Martin, himself, under rather singular and sinister circumstances— circumstances which left a never-to-be-forgotten impression on my mind.

One mild March night I left Paul's apartment with rather more than my usual irritation. I was so heated, in fact, that I determined to walk it out of my system, if possible, before retiring. As I knew by former experience, a nocturnal ramble has a quieting effect on ruffled nerves. All the poor, petty passions of man flourish best between four walls. They are soon smothered in the sable robe of outer night.

It was fine evening for a stroll. The aroma of budding spring was strong in the air—spring, that supple, green-limbed goddess whose presence is felt even in the cold, atrophied arteries of the city. A new moon hung lazily in the heavens, riding the small, silver clouds which swept past it like charging breakers. But the stars were not so fortunate. Often they were submerged beneath these foam-flecked billows of the infinite, bobbing up again into view like floating lanterns.

As I walked along toward Washington Square, the irritation, which had been so real a moment before, vanished entirely. It was followed by an almost philosophic calm. I began to take myself to task.

Why should I interfere with Paul in his choice of friends? Surely he was old enough now to choose them for himself. Just because I happened to dislike Martin, that was no reason why I should attempt to influence my brother, against him. And when it came to that, what had the fellow ever done to me that I should so hate the sound of his name? He had told me several truths hard to stomach, indeed; but no doubt they had been intended kindly as a warning. On the other hand, he had nursed me back to health when my life had hung in the balance. What had I ever done to thank him? Nothing—absolutely nothing.

Well, I would turn over a new leaf; I would apologize to Paul for what I had said.

By this time I was within a few blocks of home. Seeing an inviting alley which I had not yet explored and which might prove to be a short cut, I wandered into it and into a strange adventure as well. Winding smoothly along for several hundred yards, it was so narrow and tortuous that the old brick houses on either side seemed to be twisted out of normal shape; to be tottering toward each other like drunkards about to embrace. And then suddenly, almost violently, the alley ended in a precipitous, ivy-covered wall.

This wall brought me to an abrupt halt. I experienced a sensation of surprise, of chagrin. I had followed this alley as a man follows an odd and rather attractive philosophy, thinking that in due course it would bring me out into familiar, homely surroundings; and here was this disconcerting wall looming up like an abrupt and positive negative. I could not have been more unpleasantly surprised if a friend, while telling me a whimsical, fantastic tale, had suddenly dropped dead in the middle of a sentence. Indeed there was something brooding and brutal about this wall, like death itself.

The little street was as dark as a subterranean passageway. I might very easily have blundered into the wall without seeing it, had it not been for an antique, iron lantern which was suspended from it and which shed its flickering beams over its rough, red surface. The light, however, was not sufficient to make objects at a short distance discernable. For instance the houses on either side, and more especially their areaways, were in tottering, unstable shadow.

I came to an enforced halt near the wall and glanced at the house on my right. It seemed to me that the shadowy figure of a man was sitting on the stoop in the attitude of one who is patiently waiting; but I could not be sure of this as the mantle of gloom enshrouding the house was almost impenetrable. Whatever it was, it remained absolutely motionless.

I turned and was about to retrace my steps when I suddenly heard strange shuffling sounds. *Flip, flap, flip, flap,* the sounds grew nearer and nearer. And for some unaccountable reason I felt a flicker of fear. Through those hurrying footsteps, that flapping of worn-out leather on cobblestones, there sounded the warning of approaching danger. *Flip, flap, flip, flap*—it was like the frantic beating of terror-stricken wings.

I came to a halt and attempted to pierce the shadows in front of me. At the next moment, I stepped aside with a warning cry.

"Look out!" I shouted. "There's a wall in front of you."

But the man who ran swiftly past me, his head thrown back, his broken shoes flapping wildly on the cobblestones, could not stop himself in time. Into the wall he went at full speed; and then, rebounding like a rubber ball, toppled over on his back.

"Are you hurt?" I cried, running forward.

He was on his feet again by the time I reached him— on his feet and staring about him wildly. A ribbon of blood ran down his chin, losing itself in his grey, tangled beard; one of his knees had torn its way through the patched cloth and now projected arrogantly, a globule of raw flesh; his long, green coat, many sizes too big for him, flapped idly in the March breeze.

"Are you hurt?" I repeated, touching him on the arm.

He started and turned a pair of bloodshot eyes on me. "Oh!" he said in a husky voice. "I thought you was one of 'em! I can see you ain't now. No, mister, there ain't much wrong with me."

"But that was quite a fall you took. It must have shaken you up. Look at your knee."

"To Hell with my knee!" he cried, shaking his head like a restive horse. "I got to get out of here, mister! Ain't there a gate in this wall? For mercy's sake, get me out of here before the boss and his gang show up!"

"Who's the boss and his gang?" I asked, intending to humor him till I ascertained whether he were drunk or mad. "I'm sure everything will be all right."

"Don't you hear 'em?" he broke in, cocking his head on one side. "Don't you hear 'em? They're comin' for me now!"

Indeed I *did* hear a confused, muffled thudding in the distance which gradually grew louder, approaching with the swiftness of hurrying feet. "Probably the police," I thought to myself. "This fellow has robbed some one and is trying to make a get-a-way."

Suddenly I felt his hand on my arm. He was shaking me violently. "It's them!" he cried. "Give me a boost up on the wall, mister! Give me a leg up and I'll fool 'em yet!"

But I shook his hand from my arm. My suspicions had now become a certainty. I was not the man to help a criminal escape. I respected the laws of my country too much to see them cheated by this villainous scarecrow in his flapping green coat. If he had attempted to climb the wall, I believe I would have detained him 'till his pursuers arrived.

"You'd better stay here quietly and face the music," I said sternly. "If you break the laws, you've got to answer for it."

At that he swung away from me and limped toward one of the dark houses. "Maybe I can get in here," he muttered.

By now the thudding of a dozen pairs of feet echoed through the alley. They could not be more than a hundred yards away and they were coming fast. I saw the man stop at the bottom step of the shadowy stoop; I saw a dark figure rise slowly to its feet above him—the figure which before I had been unable to make sure of because of the gloom— and then I heard a strange conversation which I shall never be able to forget.

"Let me in your house, mister!" cried the man in the green coat. "Quick! They're comin' up the alley now! For God's sake, open the door and let me in!"

Then I heard a low laugh which rasped on my nerves like sand-paper. "I'm sorry," said a vaguely familiar voice, "but I don't happen to have the key."

What followed then is like the half-remembered figments of a dream. I saw the man in the green coat leap back as though he had come into violent contact with another wall; I heard him scream out like an animal in pain; and the next instant, he was on his knees beside me, clasping me about the waist with emaciated arms.

"Don't let 'em hurt me, mister!" he muttered. "Don't let 'em hurt me! The boss thinks I'm going to blab! Tell him—"

The rest of his words were swept away by a storm of men dashing towards us—not policemen, as I had thought, but ragged men with caps drawn down over their eyes; men flourishing cudgels, with now and then the sickly gleam of a knife flashing through them like lightning in a forest. For an instant they hovered over us like a breaking wave and then we were overwhelmed and dragged apart.

I heard a shrill scream, a dull thudding of blows falling on flesh, and then a cracking sound as though a solid substance had been shattered. At that I struggled and cried out. The next instant a sickening pain closed my eyes—I knew nothing more.

VI

When I regained consciousness it was to find myself stretched out on the pavement at the foot of the wall. Above my head, the antique iron lantern cast its feeble beams at the impenetrable ebony breast of night. I felt instinctively that some one was standing within a few feet of me, but I lacked the strength of will to sit up.

"How do you feel now?" a familiar voice asked. Turning my head with difficulty, I saw that a man stood near me, leaning up against the wall in an attitude of nonchalant unconcern. There was something in this man's air of easy indifference which was galling in the extreme. Weak as I was, I managed to sit up and rub my head.

"Oh come now, Smithers," the voice continued unfeelingly "you've been playing dead long enough. That was the merest tap you got—nothing to make a fuss about. They're all gone now. It's quite safe to stage a resurrection."

And now I knew the voice. Who but Martin could show such an utter lack of human feeling? There he stood, as indifferent as Fate, the lamp light accentuating the dark hollows under his eyes and revealing the cruel catlike curve of his lips. Like a pleased spectator at some farce, he leaned against the wall, smiling and playing absently with a small silver-headed cane.

"So it's you, Martin," I said, rising weakly to my feet. "How did you happen to find me?"

"I didn't," he answered carelessly. "On the contrary, you found me. I was sitting on the stoop of my house when you and your friend began quarreling."

"You were the man on the stoop then," I muttered. "I remember now. But what happened to that poor fellow in the green coat?"

"Your friend?" he asked.

"He was no friend of mine. I never saw him before. But what happened to him? You must have seen what happened to him?"

"He's lying over there," Martin said lightly, jerking his pointed chin over his shoulder. "And he's not *playing* dead, Smithers. You and your other friends finished him off to the queen's taste."

"My other friends?" I cried, putting my hand to my throbbing head. "Who do you mean?"

"Why, all those impulsive gentlemen who came charging down the street a few minutes ago," he answered, "those gentlemen armed with clubs. What a devil's tattoo they did play on that poor fellow's ribs! He's nothing but a bag of broken bones now, Smithers."

"They were no friends of mine!" I cried angrily.

"No?" he said, raising his eyebrows whimsically. "You seemed rather anxious to keep that poor fellow here till they had played their little game with him. If you had boosted him up on the wall, as he wanted, no doubt he'd be alive this minute."

"Surely he's not dead, Martin?" I asked with a heavy heart. "Don't tell me that he's dead!"

"As dead as a doornail," he answered laconically. "But look for yourself."

He stepped to one side and I saw something which a moment before had been hidden by his shadow. The body of the man in the green coat seemed suddenly to spring out of the gloom. There it lay, like a scarecrow which has been blown over on its face—a grotesque, inhuman figure huddled up against the wall. And from it, dark running puddles of blood crawled away, leaving strange, fern-like traceries on the dusty pavement. Yes, he was undoubtedly dead. Only the green coat seemed still alive. One of its tails stirred slightly as the strong March breeze eddied about it.

And as I looked at this pitiful broken thing which a few minutes before had been so shaken by fear, horror and remorse made me forget my aching head. Martin was right; I had held his life in my two hands and I had let it fall! Why had I not helped him to climb the wall? Why had I been so sure that the police were his pursuers? What a fool I had been! And now I could never forgive myself—never!

"Are you satisfied?" Martin asked. "Personally I should call it a rather thorough job. Look at the back of his head. Your friends, Smithers, seem to be as workmanlike as they are impulsive."

Shuddering, I turned my back on the corpse. "Please don't joke about a thing like that!" I cried. "Haven't you any mercy? I'm too sick listen to you! I feel as though I were responsible for this!"

"You are, Smithers. Don't let your natural modesty blind you to the truth. Fully two-thirds of the credit belongs to you. But you'll allow me the privilege of writing it up, won't you? I need just one more story to complete my book and this seems excellent material."

"Did you recognize any of the murderers?" I asked.

"Only you, Smithers."

"Don't joke, Martin! I mean would you recognize any of them if you should see them again?"

"No doubt," he answered carelessly. "I never forget faces. As I told you once before, my memory makes up for my lack of imagination. But I would advise you to get away before the police come. You'll be mixed up in an unpleasant affair if you don't."

"How so?"

"Well, you carried a heavy cane. Now it is broken in half. This man has been beaten to death. You are found near the body with a wound on your head."

"And you?"

"Why, I live on this street, Smithers. There is some reason why I should be here, while there is no reason under the sun why a society portrait painter should be found up a miserable, blind alley at midnight. If nothing more, it would cause considerable newspaper notoriety which I don't think would do you any good with your wealthy patrons."

"But I can't sneak out of it like this," I said weakly. "I feel that I'm too much to blame. That poor fellow might have got away if I hadn't been such a suspicious fool."

"Don't take all this so much to heart, Smithers," Martin murmured with one of his enigmatic smiles. "After all, what is one human life more or less? They are like ants, such men—only not so industrious. This fellow perished to-night in a good cause—for art's sake, indeed, for I intend to make the description of his murder a masterpiece."

"You're not human, Martin," I said, turning away. "However, I think I'll accept your advice and be off before the police come."

"I knew you would," he said triumphantly. "One can always depend on you, Smithers."

"And what are *you* going to do?"

"Why, I have modeled myself after the moon," he cried, raising his cane and pointing fantastically at the heavens. "She and I will keep watch over the dead. My cold sister, I call her. She is wise, Smithers, horribly wise—so wise, indeed, that nothing can change the sad serenity of her face. Think of what she has seen, while looking down; think of the plains dotted with the slain and the purple rivers of blood that she has seen, and then wonder at the calmness of that white face in the sky! Leave the dead to Martin and the moon, Smithers—leave them to Martin and the moon!"

I did not answer him—dizziness and nausea were stealing over me. My only thought was to escape from this dark alley before the police came. Martin's wild words seemed a fitting climax to such a ghastly business.

At the first bend in the alley I cast a hurried glance over my shoulder. Martin still stood where I had left him, his cane pointing fantastically at the moon, his eyes on the corpse which huddled close to the wall as though seeking an outlet. And the antique, iron lantern dropped its petals of pale, yellow light, like a dying sunflower, on the glistening pavement where tiny, fern-like patterns of crimson were stealing noiselessly away.

VII

For several days following my adventure in the alley, I was confined to my bed. The blow that I received had inflicted a severe scalp wound which called for medical attention; while, added to this, the unnatural excitement had brought me to the verge of a breakdown. At night I was subjected to horrible dreams from which I awoke bathed in a copious sweat.

On the day after the murder I scanned the papers eagerly. My curiosity was finally rewarded by the following paragraph:

BEATEN TO DEATH

Early this morning the body of a man was found at the foot of the wall which terminates Tyndall Place. His death was caused by the heavy blows of some blunt instrument. As yet the body has not been identified.

I laid the paper down with a sigh. So this was all the publicity the *Evening Star* thought such a ghastly business to be worth! What had shaken me to the depths of my soul, the *Evening Star* could dismiss in a few lines. I had expected to see the affair written up on the first page with perhaps a full-length picture of the man in the green coat. And I had found it only with difficulty, hidden away among the advertisements. How different it would have been had the victim possessed social prominence or even a moderate income! Then he would have come into his own on the front page in big, glaring type; a host of detectives would by now be hot on the trail of his assassins and the wheels of justice would soon be humming merrily, grinding into chaff those impulsive gentlemen, as Martin called them, who had broken simultaneously the skull of the green-coated man and the Fifth Commandment.

Martin! Evidently he had disappeared from the scene before the police arrived. Otherwise some allusion to him would have appeared in that article. No doubt he, like myself, had avoided getting himself mixed up in the affair on account of the unpleasant newspaper notoriety which was sure to follow. But why could he not have said as much to me? That was like the man—to hide his own frailties under mine; to make it appear that he was going to face the music, while in reality he was only waiting till my back was turned before he beat a hasty retreat. Well, hereafter, I would take what he said with a grain of salt. In spite of his insufferable air of egotism, he evidently had human weaknesses like the rest of us.

For the duration of that week I rested till I regained my mental and physical equilibrium. I had several callers, including Huntington, to whom I told in confidence what had befallen me in the alley. Wilbur listened with more than his customary attention, his eyes half closed and his blunt, shapeless nose twitching slightly. It was at times like these that one appreciated thoroughly the aptness of his sobriquet. Never have I seen a man who so closely resembled a guinea pig.

"Martin must be an unfeeling sort of chap," he muttered when I had finished. "You say he didn't seem to be at all disturbed by what had happened?"

"Not the least bit in the world," I assured him.

"Why, he began joking about it! You'd think he was used to seeing murders every night."

"Used to seeing murders every night!" Huntington repeated thoughtfully. "What an idea!"

"That's the impression he'd give any one. There's something not quite human about the man."

"You must bring us together, Charley," Wilbur said abruptly. "I've taken an interest in him. Psychology is my hobby, you know. Burgess Martin seems worth studying. If I weren't so infernally lazy, I'd look him up in that slum where he lives. Why was I born so lazy, Charley?"

"I don't know. Possibly you'd be a menace to society if you weren't. Your pleasing plumpness and hibernating habits are the bars of your hutch. Within, you nibble contentedly at your lettuce leaves; but, once out, you might turn carnivorous."

"A guinea pig turn carnivorous?" he said, rising. "It isn't done. But I imagine I could have much more fun with my hobby if I weren't so lazy. If crimes were committed in my back yard, I feel that I would be a famous detective. Why is it that I have a kind honest man for a valet when I long for one who has all the subtle instincts of those famous poisoners of the Renaissance?"

"Personally I should prefer the kind, honest valet, Wilbur. You can eat your lettuce leaves without the fear that they may be colored with Paris green."

"Well, at any rate, introduce me to Martin, Charley. I'm very anxious to meet him."

But Huntington was not the only one of my acquaintances who wished to meet Martin. His story, "The Murder of Mary Mortimer," had excited the interest and the admiration of a young writer who lived in the same apartment house as myself. During the last few months we had become friends; and when he learned that I had roomed with Martin in Paris, he was eager to know him.

Rupert Farrington was one of those young visionaries to be found in the bohemian quarter of any large city. Tall and slender, with large melancholy blue eyes and a girlish coloring, one had but to glance at him to realize that here was a dreamer who was incapable of crystallizing his dreams into a concrete form. There was something disconcertingly vague about his personality; one could forget his presence in the room as though he had no more mental or physical substance than a shadow. And yet, in spite of his apparent weakness, there were fiery depths in his nature capable of being roused into a storm. He loved his art passionately. Although he had never had anything accepted, he still worked on grimly with a firm belief that the editors were at fault. In fact he visualized these magazine monarchs, as he called them, as a kind of unscrupulous aristocracy which should be torn down. He spent his time writing, receiving rejection slips, and railing at the man in the editorial chair.

His voice, even when raised, impressed no one—it was like the droning of a harmless fly.

"The Murder of Mary Mortimer" still held this young man's fancy in an iron grip. He had a copy of the magazine in which it had appeared, now torn and smudged by countless readings, and I often found him poring over it when he thought he was unnoticed. He could quote whole paragraphs of it from memory; and often, when we had a studio soirée, he would be called upon for a ghastly recitation from those well-thumbed pages.

On the day following my nocturnal adventure, he dropped in to see me. As usual, he began to praise Martin to the skies. The unpleasant experience through which I had passed, coupled with the hearty detestation I entertained for my former roommate, made any allusion to the man almost unendurable. It was all I could do to keep a civil tongue in my cheek while the young fool raved.

"You seem to have Martin on the brain," I said when I could get a word in edgewise. "A man can't be called a genius just because he has written one fairly decent magazine story."

"Fairly decent!" Farrington cried, his large eyes flashing dangerously. "Why, it's a masterpiece, Smithers! It stands alone in literature! It is a picture painted with words, remorseless, vivid—"

"And extremely morbid," I broke in. "That's probably the reason he's never been able to land any of his other work. The magazine editors know that the public doesn't want to be fed up on horrors. Martin's writings, like his paintings, aren't healthy. They shouldn't be printed."

Farrington glared at me for a moment in speechless anger. In the same breath, I had committed two unpardonable offenses—I had criticized Martin's work unfavorably, and I had spoken well of magazine editors. He could not have been more thoroughly aroused if I had slapped him in the face.

"I didn't expect to hear anything like this from *you*," he said at length in a voice which he attempted to make calm. "You had the rare privilege of living with him in Paris, and yet you seem to have absorbed nothing of his Spartan philosophy. Wasn't it Oscar Wilde who said: 'There is no such thing as a moral or an immoral book. Books are well written or badly written. That is all.'"

"If I were an editor, I wouldn't publish any of his stories," I said stubbornly. "I'll make you a little bet right here and now—I bet you'll never see any more of his work in print."

"I'll take that," Farrington said, rising. "You're forgetting, Smithers, that there's another road to the public besides the magazine route. Martin's next thing may be a novel or a book of short stories."

"Perhaps," I answered, "but I'll not retract. On the contrary, I'll make another bet with you. I'll bet you that if he *does* publish anything, some day you'll wish that you hadn't wasted your time reading it."

"What do you want to bet?"

"I'll lay a hundred on both."

"All right; I'll take both," he said with a contemptuous laugh. "Martin couldn't write anything that wasn't worth reading. Good night, Smithers."

"You're young yet," I called after him. "Some day you may outgrow this silly hero-worship."

"I might live to be a thousand," he said over his shoulder, "but I'll never regret reading Martin."

Both Farrington and I were to remember those parting words of his on a certain dramatic occasion several years later. But at the time, they seemed of no more importance than the crackling of dry shells underfoot.

VIII

Although I religiously scanned the papers for the next month or so, I found no further reference to the murder of the man in the green coat. No doubt the police considered the solution of such an insignificant mystery scarcely worth their best efforts; and the press, siding with them and quite indifferent as to the fate of the victim, very obligingly let the matter drop. The old saying, "Murder will out," like many another old saying, has little or no foundation of truth. It is a matter for speculation as to how many unsolved murder mysteries, like submerged derelicts, are buried deep under the waters of time.

After my week's vacation I returned to work, refreshed in body and mind. There were several portraits which had to be finished before I received the generous checks that they were thought to be worth. For the next month I was so busy that I had no time to brood over the tragedy. However, I was not yet done with the man in the green coat, as future events proved.

One night, fully two months after my adventure, Paul dropped in to see me. He had come to find out why I had not visited him since our last altercation. I had left his house in such a rage on that never-to-be-forgotten evening that he feared an estrangement in our relations might grow out of this silly quarrel. He came to straighten matters out.

"I can't help liking the man, Charley," he said, regarding me with his steady blue eyes. "Of course, if you'd rather not have me talk about him when we are together, I won't. He seems to be an inflammatory topic of conversation between us."

"I think it just as well if we don't argue about him," I agreed. "He rubs me the wrong way, Paul."

"Then we will say nothing more about him."

"Very well."

But Paul and I were soon to realize that such a compact was impossible to keep. Hardly had we agreed to it, before the studio door was pushed violently open and Rupert Farrington strode in. His face was flushed, his hair stood on end, his eyes were shining with excitement. He flourished a volume bound in red morocco under my nose as though it were some kind of new and deadly weapon.

"I win, Smithers!" he cried excitedly. "I win!"

My first thought was that the young poet had gone mad. There he stood, coatless, collarless, hatless—a pair of pink worsted slippers adorning his flat feet, his flannel shirt open at his bony throat—waving the book about his head as though it were a tomahawk. No doubt Paul would think that such an apparition was quite a customary sight in Washington Square. I glanced at him and saw that his lips were twitching in their attempt to restrain a smile.

"You're not much of a prophet, Smithers," Farrington continued excitedly. "I told you there were more ways than one of finding recognition."

"I haven't the slightest idea what you're driving at, Rupert," I said reprovingly. "Your words and your gestures convey nothing to my mind. If you will kindly refrain from dashing my brains out with that crimson tome, I'll introduce you to my brother."

"Oh, I beg your pardon!" Farrington muttered, evidently seeing Paul for the first time. "Glad to meet you, I'm sure. This book got me so worked up that I'm not quite myself."

"I'm very pleased to meet you," Paul murmured in the tone of a man saying: "Oh, don't mind me! I know this is bohemia—so be just as wild as you want."

"Now sit down, Rupert," I continued, "and explain what you mean. You say that you win. *What* do you win? You say that I am a poor prophet. When did I ever prophesy to you?"

Farrington seated himself and smiled triumphantly. "I win a hundred dollars from you," said he. "And I win it, because you made a false prophecy about Burgess Martin."

Paul and I started and interchanged glances. We had just agreed to drop the man's name from our conversation; yet here it was, popping up again with the obstinacy of a cork submerged for an instant under water! Evidently we could not so easily dismiss him from our intercourse as we had imagined.

"What has Burgess Martin to do with it?" I asked sharply.

"Everything," Farrington replied. "His book, 'Many Murders,' is being brought out by the Brainsworth

Publishing Company next week. I have an advance copy which Williamson of the *Evening Star* loaned me. I believe you made a little bet, Smithers, that Martin wouldn't get any more of his work into print. I brought this book along as proof."

As he finished, he handed me the volume bound in red morocco. I had a feeling of extreme irritation as I examined it—an irritation which did not spring solely from the fact that I had just lost a bet. Any allusion to Martin was like the lash of a whip falling on my sensitive self-pride.

"So he has succeeded in having his work published at last," I muttered.

"And I feel that it will be a classic!" Paul cried enthusiastically.

"Don't be too sure of that," I replied. "It's more likely to be highly sensational melodrama. 'Many Murders!' Why, the thing bears the hallmark of the dime novel!"

Farrington flushed angrily. "You're wrong, Smithers," said he. "The Brainsworth Publishing Company doesn't bring out dime novels."

"But I presume you'll acknowledge that even the Brainsworth Publishing Company can make mistakes. We'll see what the critics have to say about it."

Farrington burst out into a laugh. "That's like you, Smithers. You'd never acknowledge anything was good till a band of learned asses told you so. Have you ever heard of Sir Vivian Gerard?"

"The famous London critic? Of course! Who hasn't?"

"Well, the Brainsworth Publishing Company sent the manuscript of 'Many Murders' to him for his opinion. He wrote a glowing review of it which they are now using for advertising purposes. Here's a selection from it which they enclosed with each review copy."

Farrington fumbled in his pocket and drew out a small wrinkled sheet of printed matter. Adjusting his spectacles on his bony nose, he began to read the review. It ran as follows:

A MASTER OF HORROR

It gives me great pleasure to introduce to the world an undoubted master of the horror tale. Not since the days of Poe has America produced such a consummate craftsman. I do not hesitate to say that even the immortal creator of "The Gold Bug" had not the power of description which makes Burgess Martin's work unforgettable.

"Many Murders"—Mr. Martin's first book—is a masterpiece of the terrible. Simple, direct, quite free from any attempt to mystify the reader, each one of these weird sketches stands out like a finely carved cameo. While reading them, one thrills to a sensation of the actual. It is almost as though the reader were an eyewitness of those scenes which have flowed so vividly from their creator's fertile imagination. Morbid they may be; but, for all that, they deserve a lasting place in modern fiction.

"What have you got to say to that, Charley?" Paul cried.

"Not a thing," I answered a trifle shamefacedly. "When Sir Vivian Gerard makes such a statement, it not for me to contradict. Have you read the book, Rupert?"

"Yes," said Farrington enthusiastically. "I read it last night and I couldn't get to sleep till morning. There's one sketch in it which I think is even better than 'The Murder of Mary Mortimer.'"

"What's that?" Paul asked.

"He calls it 'In a Blind Alley.' It's the last sketch in the book."

"What's the theme?" I inquired with a sudden suspicion of the truth.

"It hasn't a plot or any conventional theme," Farrington replied rather contemptuously. "The narrator sees a man beaten to death by a band of thugs. There's a kind of bitter irony running through it. The victim pleads with the narrator to help him over the high brick wall which terminates the street—his pursuers are right on his heels, you understand—but the narrator is a conventional fool who, because the victim wears rags, thinks that he must be a crook trying to escape from the police. He refuses to help; a crowd of thugs dash up and it's all over with the poor devil. By the way, Smithers, that chap who wouldn't help the other reminds me of you."

"Thanks," I murmured with a wildly beating heart. "Perhaps I would have acted so under the same circumstances. But I don't see anything remarkable about that story."

"It isn't the theme!" cried Farrington impatiently. "It's the way it's treated. Why, you can see the whole thing— the obstinate stone wall partly illumined by an antique lantern; the poor, cowering wretch, on his hands and knees, begging for mercy; and then the mob, with their cudgels, approaching like a many-headed monster. But the death of the man in the green coat! How vivid that is! You can

see him squirming beneath a forest of clubs, you can hear
the dull thudding blows! And when it's all over, when the
many-headed monster crawls back into its lair, you have
a vivid impression of the scene—the body crumpled up
against the wall, the moon peering down with her enigmatic
smile, and the conventional fool striding off before the
police come, to avoid unpleasant notoriety."

"And what happened to Martin?" I cried out incau-
tiously. "Didn't he sneak away, too?"

"Martin?" said Paul. "Why, what do you mean,
Charley? This is only a story!"

"To be sure," I said with a forced laugh. "Rupert told
it so vividly that it made me forget. Lend me the book, will
you?"

"Certainly, Smithers," Farrington answered, eyeing me
curiously. "I'll be very glad to have you read it. At last you
seem to be interested in Martin. You'd better read it to-night
while you're in the right mood."

I acted on his suggestion. After he and Paul had
gone, I took up "Many Murders" and turned to the last
story. There it was, my adventure in the alley, so vivid, so
remorseless, that it was as though I were living once again
those terrible moments. And as I read on, great drops of
sweat gathered on my forehead—gathered there and trickled
down into my smarting eyes. Martin had indeed succeeded
in painting a picture with words.

IX

"Many Murders" set the whole literary world agog for several months. Critical articles concerning it appeared in all the leading newspapers and magazines. It is to be noted that none of these referred to it as an average work of fiction. No, this volume of sketches was called a masterpiece or else the sensational nightmare of a disordered brain.

Soon the public became excited and bought the book by the thousands, thereby proving that Martin had been right when he had said that his stories would prove popular. Sir Vivian Gerard wrote an article for one of the periodicals in which he claimed that it was the first classic to become a best-seller immediately after publication.

Farrington kept me well posted as to the success of Martin's book. Not contented with winning his bet, he had an irritating way of gloating over my discomfiture. If "Many Murders" had been his own work, he could not have taken a greater pride in its reception by the world.

He would drop into the studio of an evening with a laudatory criticism of the book. "Well, when will you acknowledge that you have lost the other bet too, Smithers?" he would ask.

"What other bet?"

"Why, the bet you made the other day that at some future date I would regret having read Martin's work."

"Oh, I'd forgotten about it. But I won't have to pay that bet for a long time. You might regret having read Martin's work when you were on your deathbed."

"Don't be a piker, Smithers. Name some definite date."

"Oh, very well. Let's say about twenty years from now."

"You *are* a piker, Smithers. But have it your own way."

I saw very little of Martin during the months which followed the publication of his book. Sometimes I met him at Paul's apartment where, in spite of the fact that he was now one of the shining literary lights of the world, he was a frequent visitor. Naturally I avoided him whenever I could. Beside my inherent repulsion for the man which had grown since our adventure in the alley, I felt instinctively that he was laughing inwardly to see his prophecy about my career turning out to be so true.

One bright October afternoon, Paul and Martin paid me a visit. As chance would have it, the studio door stood ajar and they entered without the formality of a knock. At the moment was retouching a portrait of Mrs. Vanderveer, a prominent figure in the society world, and was so intent on my work that I did not notice their presence till Martin spoke.

"And who is that supposed to be?" he asked in his cold impersonal way.

At the sound of his voice I started like a guilty schoolboy. "Mrs. Vanderveer," I muttered. "But it isn't finished yet."

"Really?" said he. "I've known her for some time. My sight must be failing."

"No, it's not that!" I cried bitterly. "I know it looks no more like her than her own daughter! But a man must live!"

Martin eyed me ironically and his lips curled up at the corners. "That's what people think down on my street," he murmured. "It's a fine old saying, and many a brave man has adorned the end of a rope because of it."

"Cut out the shop talk!" Paul broke in, seeing the embarrassment and hot anger written on my face. "Burgess and I are going on a little trip to the Maine woods. We've both got a vacation coming to us."

"When do you leave?" I asked, turning my back on Martin.

"Saturday morning. It will be corking in the woods now. We should get some good shooting. Why don't you join us, Charley?"

"No, I've a lot of work on hand. I've got to finish five portraits by Christmas. Remember me, Paul, if you get a buck and smuggle a few nice steaks back with you. You know how I like venison."

Although I was not looking at Martin when I refused Paul's invitation, I felt instinctively that he was pleased to know that I would not accompany them. And so what was my surprise when he seconded my brother's proposal. There was a genuine ring in his voice which I had never heard before.

"You'd better come, Smithers," he said. "An artist should find delight in the woods at this time of year. The foliage will be ablaze with color. You'll regret it if you don't come, Smithers."

I stared at him in amazement. There was a propitiatory air about the man, quite foreign to his usual manner. It was almost as though he were pleading with me to go.

What possible reason could he have for applying balm to my wounded sensibilities at this late date? Well, I would give him a taste of his own medicine—I would show him, once and for all, that I was not the sort of man one could take liberties with and then expect to jog along behind at a kind word like a whipped dog. He might have won the fawning flattery of the world, but he could not win my esteem if he were the most masterful writer of all time. What was a genius, after all, but a mental abnormality—a creature bordering on insanity and tolerated only because it could amuse? Was not a keen, capable man of affairs on a far higher plane? Healthy thought, irrespective of its originality, to my mind, at least, was preferable to those brilliant poisonous inspirations which sprout from the oozing mire without apparent source and are called the fruits of genius.

"No, Martin," I said coldly, "your blazing, autumnal foliage does not tempt me. As you have often said, I am preëminently a society portrait painter who takes more pleasure in rustling bank-notes than in rustling leaves. I've got to stay here and stick to business."

His long, lean face which had worn a strange, almost wistful expression, suddenly stiffened into its habitual sneering aloofness. "Very well, Smithers," he said quietly. "Have it your own way. Stay home and stick to business. Let's be going, Paul."

"I'm sorry you won't come with us, Charley," Paul said, gripping my hand in leavetaking. "I'll not forget what you said about venison. We'll be back in two months, Charley."

X

After they had left the studio, I strode to one of the windows and looked out. A moment later I saw them on the street. They were walking side by side. As never before, the contrast between the two men caused me a sensation of amazement. Paul was so flushed with health, so alive, so virile; Martin, gliding beside him with a catlike tread, his sallow face turned toward me, was so ethereal by comparison, so ghostlike, so unwholesome! It was as though Life and Death were walking in the bright October sunshine.

"That man is like an evil shadow," I muttered. "What can Paul see in him? Surely they won't stay up in the woods for two months. Paul will grow tired of it before then and come home."

Several days after Paul and Martin had left the city, I went out of town for a week-end with Wilbur Huntington. He had a country place on Long Island; and we spent Saturday, Sunday, and the better part of Monday, sauntering about a nearby golf course and sipping cool drinks afterward in the shade of the veranda.

On Monday afternoon Wilbur insisted on driving me into town in his racing car. I arrived at the studio in due course, wind-swept and dusty, with the dazed feeling of one who has been shot through space with the velocity of a falling star. Huntington's laziness did not extend to his motor. He had entered it in the Vanderbilt Cup and I was confident that afternoon that it had every chance of winning.

I was attempting to get some of the Long Island dust out of my eyes, when I heard a loud knocking on the studio door. "Come in," I shouted. "I'm washing up. I'll be there in a moment."

My caller proved to be Rupert Farrington. He did not wait for me to complete my ablutions, but hurried into the bathroom and handed me a telegram.

"It came while I was at lunch," he explained. "You told me that you'd be home for dinner, so I signed the book for you."

"I'm much obliged," I answered, drying my hands. "It's probably from Mrs. Dyer. She's been pestering me to death about having her portrait finished before Christmas. This will be her third telegram."

"It must be a wonderful feeling to know that one is so necessary to society at large," Rupert said unpleasantly. "You're a lucky dog, Smithers. But I've got to be going. Drop in and see me when art's not beckoning."

I made a rather careful toilet before I opened the yellow envelope. Telegrams were no novelty to me. I had learned by bitter experience that a certain class of women send them with no more urgent reason than so many children scribbling notes behind their teacher's back.

At last strode back into the studio where the red light from the setting sun touched one of the canvases as though with fire. Striding to the window, I tore open the telegram and glanced at it. The next instant it fluttered from my hand to the floor.

"Good God!" I muttered.

Unconsciously I looked down at the piece of yellow paper which lay in a band of crimson light that seemed to stain it as though with blood. The black letters leaped up from it into my brain. Once more I read their purport:

Paul is dead. Am bringing him home on the four-fifteen.

Martin

"Paul is dead," I repeated. But it meant nothing to me then—nothing! It seemed as impossible as the wildest dream. Like a tongue-tied actor attempting to make his lines clear and convincing, I repeated those few words over and over again: "Paul is dead—Paul is dead."

But still that thin partition standing between me and the realization of the truth, resisted the dull pounding of those hammerlike words. And suddenly a brain-numbing fear stole over me, a fear that I could never be more than a puppet which had been wound up to repeat endlessly that meaningless phrase: "Paul is dead."

"Come now!" I told myself. "You must make yourself realize what this telegram means. You must suffer. It is right that you should suffer. Other men would suffer in your place. Can you not understand? Paul is dead!"

But still that thin partition was standing bravely against those hammerlike words. And wonderingly, fearfully, like a child in the dark, I looked out over the city.

XI

The sun was slowly setting far away over those dingy housetops which were like uneven stepping-stones above the murmur of a brook. The sky hung over them like a sea of blood dotted here and there with floating islands of ice. Somewhere in the distance the shrill voice of a siren drifted, melancholy, forlorn, tearing its way like a projectile through a muttering multitude of other sounds. Surely it was pain incarnate—pain which I sought and which evaded me.

And as I gazed wonderingly at the passionate sky, a thought edged its way into my benumbed brain. Surely it was after five o'clock. What was it that this yellow, wrinkled piece of paper at my feet warned me of? Something which Martin was bringing home on the four-fifteen. It was already an hour past that time. But what was this inanimate thing of which he spoke? Why, it was Paul—my brother Paul, dead, already cold—Paul who had joked and laughed with me, who had fought and forgiven me—Paul!

And like a weary swimmer who has dived from a high cliff into the sea, slowly true realization fought its way up through the dark depths. I was no longer a mere puppet, squeaking a meaningless phrase. Pain was born in an instant—blinding, unbearable pain.

Paul was dead! I, who had known him so intimately, who had loved him so dearly, realized that fully now. Striding to and fro, quite careless of the furniture which stood in my way, hearing nothing, seeing nothing, knowing nothing but, this unforgettable fact, I was driven back and forth by the painful lash of memory like a wild animal in its cage.

I do not know how long I wandered aimlessly about the room. Suddenly I was brought to normal consciousness by loud knocking on the studio door.

"Come in," I muttered. "Come in."

The door opened and Martin strode swiftly into the room. In spite of my abnormal mental condition, I could not help noticing his altered appearance. The man seemed to have grown years older in those few short days. His face was heavily lined and as gray as a death's head; the whites of his eyes were threaded with tiny crimson veins as though from prolonged weeping; and his voice was as hoarse as the cawing of a crow.

"How's this?" he asked. "Didn't you get my telegram?"

I pointed mutely to where it lay on the floor and once more began to pace the room.

"Well, why didn't you meet me?" he cried angrily. "But it's like you to dodge all your responsibilities!"

"Where is Paul?" I asked dully.

"I've had him taken to his apartment. Go there and you'll find him."

"I'll go right away," I said weakly. "Wait till I get my hat."

"Don't you want to know how he was killed?" he cried in a kind of rage. "I bring your only brother home dead and you treat the whole affair as a matter of course! Why, common curiosity should prompt you to ask a few questions!"

"You don't understand me, Martin," I said with a brave attempt at dignity. "What do I care about such details now? He's dead—that's all I care to know. Later, perhaps. Poor old Paul! If I'd gone with him—"

But Martin interrupted me with a quick, authoritative gesture. "Listen, Smithers," he ordered. "It happened this way: Our guide had a gallon of whisky. Paul began drinking again heavily. You know how it was when the stuff was in reach; he simply couldn't resist it. I tried to reason with him, but it wasn't any use. After the whisky was all gone, he had an attack of melancholia. You remember how depressed he used to get after a drinking bout at college?"

"Yes," I muttered.

"Well, this time it was far worse. He refused to be dragged out of the depths. One night the guide and I awoke with the sound of a gunshot in our ears. We ran out of the cabin to find Paul lying on the ground."

"Dead?"

"I should think so!" Martin answered brutally. "Why, he had a hole in his side that you could stick your arm into!"

The coroner bore out Martin's statement in regard to Paul's death. There was no doubt that the poor fellow, suffering from acute melancholia, had taken his own life. Tying a piece of string about the trigger of his shotgun, he had leaned his weight upon the muzzle and discharged it by pressing his foot down hard upon the loose, dangling cord. His death must have been almost instantaneous. The heavy buckshot had ripped its way through his heart.

My mother was prostrated by the news. Ever since father's death she had been in poor health, and this was the last straw. On the day of the funeral she was so weak that the doctor refused to allow her to leave her bed. I was the only member of the family to attend the solemn ceremony. But Wilbur Huntington, although he knew Paul only slightly, was kind enough to accompany me.

It was one of those dismal days in late autumn, I remember—a day when all nature is solemn, melancholy, as though mourning for the wasteful abandonment of her youth. A gray drizzle of rain was falling which seemed to curtain us off from the outer world. Like strange, solemn ships, the funeral procession drifted slowly toward its goal.

Our snail's pace through the glistening streets grated on my overtaxed nerves. I had a wild impulse to shout to the man on the box, to order him to whip up his horses and drive us faster.

Suddenly Huntington's voice broke in upon my thoughts. "When a man takes a bitter dose of medicine, he takes it in a hurry. He doesn't sip it for the tastes, does he?"

"No," I answered, at a loss for his meaning.

"Then why all this?" he asked, pointing at my black clothes. "And why is it that we can't rattle along the streets at a livelier pace?"

"Custom," I explained.

"Custom be damned! The decent, sensible thing is to hide one's inner feelings from the world—not to parade them through the streets, as we are doing now, for the mob to gibber at. A funeral procession is a relic of barbarism; and there goes another."

We were entering the cemetery as he spoke, and the dull tolling of a bell rang out on the still air. Like the beating of a grief-stricken heart, solemnly, sadly, it uttered its message of misery to the living. And on every side, where tiny crosses held out their weary arms, where tombstones seemed kneeling phantoms, where long flat slabs of granite crouched like lizards, a sad echo seemed to rise and steal away on noiseless wings.

"All this," Huntington continued, "your friend Martin would very truly call toys made for the mass-mind. They hide true feeling and, like wine, intensify the emotions. But here we are."

"Poor old Paul!" I murmured.

The carriage came to a halt and we got out. Soon a number of my brother's friends assembled at the open grave and the simple service was well under way. Once, moved by an unaccountable impulse, I turned my head and saw Martin standing directly behind me. His face was as expressionless as though it had been hewn out of marble; his bloodshot eyes were staring straight at the coffin.

At last the ceremony was over. Now two men were filling up the grave with damp earth which fell on the lid of the casket with a dismal, reverberating sound. It was at this moment that I heard Martin speak in a low, muffled voice which seemed to come from deep down underground.

"It is done!" he murmured.

"What is done?" I asked in a low voice. "Surely, for Paul, it is just the beginning."

"I have buried my heart with your brother," he said. But there was a strange exultation in his tone which scarcely tallied with his words. I saw Huntington glance at him curiously.

XII

After Paul's funeral, Martin passed out of my life completely. Occasionally Rupert Farrington would refer to him in glowing terms and prophesy that he would soon startle the world with another gruesome masterpiece. But, at these times, I was careful to lend a deaf ear to his eulogies.

Poor Farrington! I grew very attached to him as the years went by. He was one of those unfortunate mortals who have the inclination to do big things in art and yet never have the ability to perform them. A tongue-tied dreamer, he would have starved years before, if his father had not sent him a generous allowance. And it was a pitiful thing to see him circling round and round the flame of genius with no hope of gaining the inner sanctuary—a poor moth doomed to outer darkness, struggling for recognition till his wings were singed.

Day after day he fought valiantly to compose one stirring line; day after day, bitter disappointment was his lot.

Like many another man of his type, he could not criticize what he had written. To him, each poem was good—perhaps a masterpiece. The editors were at fault. They could not recognize genius when they saw it. Hatred of them had become an over-mastering obsession. He would rail against them till he grew purple in the face.

I remember distinctly one Christmas morning, a month before Martin's second book came out. Rupert broke in on me while was having breakfast, his eyes wild and staring, his face suffused with blood. Stamping up and down the room, he gave vent to such a blind, ungovernable fit of fury that I feared for his reason.

"What's the trouble?" I asked when I could make myself heard.

"Trouble?" he fairly shouted. "Trouble? I'd like to wring his damn neck!"

"Whose neck?"

"Why, Hubbard's neck—Hubbard of the *Firefly*."

"What's he done to you?" I asked mildly.

Farrington came to an abrupt halt and fixed his blazing eyes on my face. "I'll tell you what he's done," he said in a voice which he attempted to make calm but which trembled on a sob. "Do you remember my last poem, 'The Sea-Gull'? Well, it was a pretty smooth piece of work, although you didn't seem to appreciate it."

"What has 'The Sea-Gull' got to do with Hubbard?" I inquired.

"I sent it to him for his magazine," he answered bitterly. "That was a month ago. They've had it ever since. I thought that I'd landed something at last. What's to-day, Smithers?"

"To-day? Why, it's Christmas morning."

"To be sure—Christmas morning! Well, I got it back in the first mail, tied up with red ribbons. Now maybe you think that's a joke, Smithers—a damn good joke?"

"No, I don't," I hastened to assure him.

"Well, I don't either," said Farrington grimly. "I've worked too hard for that. It seems to me a contemptible thing to do—a low-down, contemptible thing! To keep it so long that I had hope and then to send it back tied up with red ribbons on Christmas day! I wish I had him here, that's all! I could beat him to death without the slightest compunction. A man who would do such a thing, *should* be beaten to death! Why, Smithers, I tell you it—"

"But how do you know that Hubbard is responsible for this?" I broke in. "It sounds more like one of his office force to me—some silly little stenographer playing a practical joke."

But Farrington shook his head stubbornly. "No, it was Hubbard—undoubtedly it was Hubbard. It's his kind of humor. Have you ever seen the man? Have you ever talked to him?"

"No."

"Well, he's a pompous jelly bag with a silly, secretive smile—a sly man and a cruel man, a man who sits in his office like a round-bellied spider waiting to pounce on the flies. He makes game of us, Smithers—we poor fellows who try so hard and get so little! But he and his kind are driving me too hard! There are things that I won't stand, things that—"

"I think you're mistaken, Rupert," I broke in. "Calm yourself. This magazine proposition is driving you dotty. What possible reason could Hubbard have for doing such a thing?"

"Oh, just a little recreation," Rupert muttered. "His humor has to be tickled ever so often. But he's driving me too far, Smithers—a damn sight too far!"

I did not see Farrington again for several days. I was called out of town on an important business engagement; and when I returned, it was to find that he had gone home for the week-end.

One night, ten days later, I walked past his door and noticed that it was ajar. Glancing in, I saw Rupert seated in his favorite rocking-chair. As usual, when alone, he wore a faded brown smoking jacket and crimson worsted slippers. But to-night there was something incongruous about the man which drew my attention. Perhaps it was the rigid way he sat, or perhaps it was natural curiosity to learn what had transpired since I had seen him last, but something prompted me to enter. Glancing at him again, as I did so, I noticed a volume bound in red morocco resting on the arm of his chair.

"Rupert," I said, "what have you been doing with yourself?"

But he did not answer me. Silent, immovable, he sat staring into space.

"What's the matter with you, Rupert?" I said in a louder tone. "You're not sick, are you?" I bent forward and touched him on the shoulder.

At that, he started and looked up. His eyes were bloodshot, the veins on his forehead were black and bulging, his thick red lips were extended in animal pout.

"What's the trouble?" he said thickly. "Is that you, Smithers?"

By this time I was thoroughly alarmed. "You're not sick, are you?" I repeated shaking him by the arm. "What's the matter, Rupert?"

"Matter?" he repeated dazedly, shaking his head as though to rid himself of an unpleasant thought. "There's nothing the matter, Smithers. I've been thinking, that's all."

"You were in a kind of coma when I first came in."

He laughed a trifle shamefacedly it seemed to me. "Thoughts carry me away sometimes," he said in a more natural tone. "They drag my ego out of my body by the hair." He paused and ran his hand across his forehead. "At least, Martin's thoughts do," he finished with a faint smile.

"Martin's thoughts? Has his new book come out yet? Is that it?" I pointed to the red morocco volume on the arm of his chair.

"Yes, that's his new book," Rupert answered. "This is another advance copy. I believe it is to be published in a few days."

"What's the title?"

"'The Confessions of Constantine.'"

"Do you like it as well as 'Many Murders'?"

"*Like* it?" he cried with a nervous start. "That's scarcely the word, Smithers. You can't *like* a book of this kind—you can only marvel at it!"

"Own up now, Rupert," I said quickly, thinking that the man was quibbling to defend his idol. "Own up, this book has fallen below your expectations. In a word, it disappoints you."

"Good Lord, no!" he cried almost fiercely. "If 'Many Murders' were a masterpiece, 'The Confessions of Constantine' is a super-masterpiece! It is so great that one fears it; so great that it conquers one's mind! Can there be such a thing as hypnotic writing, Smithers?"

"Of course not," I answered irritably. "The trouble with you is that you're mentally sick. What you need is a long vacation somewhere. Why don't you go home for a month or so?"

"Perhaps I will," he muttered. "Perhaps I will." He picked up the book and began to turn the leaves. "I know I ought to go home," he added a trifle wistfully.

"Have you forgiven Hubbard yet?" I asked, turning toward the door. "Or have you found out that he wasn't responsible for that Christmas present?"

But Farrington did not answer me. Evidently he had once more become engrossed in Martin's new book. Oblivious to everything about him, he sat with a strange, rigid attention, slowly turning the leaves. And, as I glanced back at him over my shoulder, it seemed to me that his face suddenly underwent a change—that the whites of his eyes were suffused with blood; that the veins in his forehead became black and bulging; that his moist, red lips puffed out at each long breath. And I left him thus, alone with "The Confessions of Constantine."

XIII

Martin's new book was published the following week. If his first volume had caused a breeze of public comment, his second created a whirlwind. Those who were unfortunate enough to have read "The Confessions of Constantine" before it was suppressed by the government, can still remember the terrifying sensations with which it inspired them. Sir Vivian Gerard aptly phrased it in a newspaper article which ended in these words:

> I trembled when I read "Many Murders" as though I were actually witnessing the terrible crimes which it described; but when I perused "The Confessions of Constantine," my hand was steady and my brain on fire with the blood lust of the murderer as he strikes the fatal blow. I felt no repulsion at the savagery of it; only the great, unholy joy of brute rage. I cannot criticize this book; I can only wonder at it.

It was shortly after "The Confessions of Constantine" made its appearance that the still well-remembered crime wave swept New York from end to end. The police fought valiantly to hold it in check, but failed. In vain they made countless arrests; new murderers sprang up on all sides. It was as though it were some kind of contagious disease—a "murder microbe" as some learned fool maintained.

One afternoon, while this dangerous plague was at its height, Wilbur Huntington dropped into the studio on his way to the Cap and Gown Club. I was delighted to see him and stopped work for a time to chat.

"Well, what do you think of this murder scourge we're having?" I asked, laying my brush aside.

"It's rather interesting, don't you think?" he said, half closing his eyes. "I see you have a new bolt on your door, Charley."

"Yes," I answered, flushing slightly. "One has to nowadays. Bolts and locks are the fashion. They tell me the chief of police has himself guarded like a feudal baron."

"Strange that everyone should be murdering some one," Huntington continued, his nose twitching slightly. "But seriously, Charley, the baffling fact about these crimes is the manner in which they are perpetrated."

"What do you mean?"

"I mean just that. A man goes out and murders someone without any real reason and without any skill. Murder is committed everywhere these days; and no one seems to care whether he's found out or not. Murder used to be shrouded in mystery; now it walks brazenly in the sunlight, inviting the attention of any passer-by. Do you know how many murderers gave themselves up last week?"

"No. How many?"

"Forty-nine. Forty-nine out of fifty! And they all seem proud of it! That's strange, isn't it, Charley?"

"Yes, it is," I answered. "It would seem that Professor Knolls might be right about the murder microbe."

Huntington threw back his head and laughed. "No, I think not, Charley," he said. "But what does your friend Martin say about all this?"

"How should *I* know? I haven't seen him now in nearly two years."

"You haven't, eh?" Huntington settled back on the lounge and closed his eyes. "What's the matter with that Farrington fellow?" he asked after a pause.

"Nothing, that I know of. Why?"

"I just met him as I was coming up the street. He seemed to be in a devilish hurry—his face red as a beet, his eyes staring. He looked as if he had gone dotty. I shouted to him, but he didn't seem to hear me—just went scooting by on those long legs of his. He left me staring, I can tell you."

"Rupert hasn't been himself lately," I hastened to explain. "You've got to make allowances for the poor fellow. All his life he's tried to become a famous poet and he's no further advanced now than he was ten years ago."

"That's a shame!" Huntington muttered. "I never knew he had worked so hard. Isn't there anything we could do for him—bribe some publisher to bring out his poems, for instance?"

"I'm afraid that wouldn't do any good," I answered. "You see, he really hasn't got the stuff. It would be a mistaken kindness. What he ought to do, would be to—"

"Who's that laughing in the hallway?" Huntington broke in suddenly. "That's a devil of a racket! Have you got a crazy man about the premises?"

"I don't hear anything. You must be mistaken."

But Huntington cautioned me to silence with a lifted finger. "Listen!" he whispered.

Then I heard it. And what a laugh it was, starting deep down in the throat in a kind of horrid chuckling and rising higher and higher till it ended in a dismal howl! Nearer and nearer it came, rising and falling, battering on the eardrums with a savage insistency. Finally the studio door flew open and we caught a glimpse of him who laughed.

Rupert Farrington stood on the threshold, swaying back and forth as though shaken by that inhuman merriment which tore his lips apart. His face was a deep crimson; beneath the flushed skin, all the muscles were aquiver like a handful of worms. But the man's eyes were what caused me to utter an ejaculation of dismay. The pupils seemed mere pinpoints while the areas of white had grown enormous and were threaded with vivid veins. And as one looked at those eyes, a strange transformation seemed to take place; they were no longer eyes but spiders—spiders crouching in a crimson web.

I ran forward and took his arm. "What's the matter, Rupert?" I cried. "What's wrong with you?"

But he continued to shake with laughter—laughter which made every muscle in his body writhe as though in pain.

"What's the matter?" I repeated. "Are you mad? Stop that laughing or I'll shake it out of you! Haven't you any self-control?"

But still he laughed, painfully, immoderately, with his head thrown back and his eyes staring vacantly at the ceiling. Apparently he did not hear me.

Now Wilbur Huntington took a hand in the game. Stepping forward with unwonted briskness, he tapped Rupert on the chest with a commanding forefinger. "Burgess Martin wants to know what you think of 'The Confessions of Constantine,'" he said in a loud, authoritative voice. "Do you hear what I am saying, Rupert Farrington? Burgess Martin wants to know what you think of 'The Confessions of Constantine.'"

Then a strange thing happened. Rupert's discordant laughter died away. It was as though it had been bottled up in his throat. His bloodshot eyes left the ceiling and became fixed on Huntington's face.

"Tell him I like it," he said thickly. "Tell him it's true—damn true! A dull knife makes no difference—even a paper cutter will serve. To have one beneath you whom you hate; and then to strike—to strike not once or twice but a hundred times!"

Farrington raised one of his long arms above his head and I saw with horror that his coat-sleeve was stained with blood.

"Tell Burgess Martin that I have read 'The Confessions of Constantine' over and over again," he continued in a singsong voice. "Tell him that I have often crept into its pages. It is such a small book; yet I feel that I can find my way into it at will. That door is never locked. It opens readily. Sometimes before one knows it, one is inside. This afternoon I took a walk with 'The Confessions of Constantine.' We walked till I met a man who should not live—an editor who should not live!"

"He means Hubbard of the *Firefly*," I whispered to Huntington. "Do you think he has—"

But Farrington broke in upon me. He had lifted his voice to a shout. "The book opened its leaves to me, you understand. I entered a small room. He was sitting with his back turned toward me. There was an inviting ripple of flesh above his collar. Like a luscious bun it bulged out anxiously to receive the knife's sharp kiss. I hated this man and I approached. But did I hate him after all? Ah, no. Surely I loved him with a great if transitory love! Does the butcher hate the sheep that is bleating in its death agonies? Does the tiger hate the fawn which has fallen to its lot? Surely it is not hatred which makes us kill, but *love*—love for—"

Farrington broke off suddenly. The color receded from his face; his eyes seemed to be covered with a thin coating of glass. He swayed forward.

"Catch him!" Huntington cried sharply. "He's going off into a swoon!"

Hardly had he spoken before Rupert fell into my arms. He was a light man, and I had no difficulty in supporting him to the lounge where he promptly collapsed into a senseless heap of humanity. Then I turned to Wilbur with a dawning suspicion of the truth.

"What did he mean?" I cried. "Do you think he has killed anyone?"

Huntington nodded grimly. "I shouldn't wonder," he muttered. "Who was the man in the room? Has he quarreled with an editor?"

"Yes and no. He thinks he has a grudge against Hubbard of the *Firefly*. But it was nothing serious—nothing to make a man commit murder."

Wilbur shook his head. "That doesn't seem to matter nowadays. Murders are committed for the merest trifles. Yesterday an old chap killed his housekeeper because she forgot to put sugar on his grapefruit. Did you know that Farrington was quoting from 'The Confessions of Constantine' just before he caved in?"

"No, I didn't. I haven't read the book."

"Well, he was. I remember the passage distinctly. It's the most unpleasant thing in the whole damn book. It's a description of a murder which is supposed to be written by the murderer himself; and while you're reading it, you feel that you're sticking the knife in with your own hand!"

"Do you think Rupert's insane?"

"I don't know. It seems to me more like a fit—or a hypnotic trance. The man was not responsible for what he did, that's certain. But I'm going to look into this new book of Martin's—by Heaven, I am!"

For some time longer we talked in lowered voices with an occasional side-long look at Farrington who had apparently sunk into a deep sleep. The young poet lay on his back—one of his hands dangled nearly to the floor; the other rested on his breast, protruding from the bloodstained coat-sleeve like a white flower from an earthen jug. His small, rather girlish face had regained its habitual calm; now a smile hovered about the lips.

"I shouldn't wonder if he awoke in his right mind," Huntington whispered.

At that moment, Rupert opened his large, melancholy eyes. "Where am I?" he murmured.

"It's all right," I hastened to assure him. "You're in my studio. You've been sick, Rupert."

"Sick?" he repeated. "I had a terrible dream. I thought I had killed Hubbard and that I had actually enjoyed doing it." He smiled weakly.

"Don't talk too much," Huntington warned him.

"You're still very weak. You'll need your strength later. Why, what's the matter?"

"My God!" Farrington muttered. His wandering eyes had rested for an instant on his coat-sleeve. Staring at the bloodstained cuff, he repeated dully: "My God! It's true then—all true!"

"Oh, probably you've just cut your wrist a bit," Huntington said kindly.

"No, it all comes back to me now," Farrington cried, moistening his lips with his tongue. "I had been reading 'The Confessions of Constantine' and somehow I had lost my identity in those pages. *I* didn't murder Hubbard—it was someone else who had climbed into my body while my soul was asleep; some red, roaring beast from 'The Confessions of Constantine'! I know that you fellows can't understand what I mean! You think I'm trying to get out of this, but I'm not! I'm willing to pay the price!"

"Hush," said Huntington, "I hear footsteps in the corridor."

Suddenly the sound of heavy knocking echoed through the room. Someone was pounding on the studio door.

"Come in," I called.

Now the door swung slowly open and two policemen stepped into the room. Glancing about curiously, their eyes finally rested on Farrington.

"Well?" said Huntington sharply.

"Is Mr. Farrington here?" the taller policeman asked.

Rupert rose and confronted them. "That's my name," he said quietly. "What do you want of me?"

"You're wanted for the murder of. J. E. Hubbard, editor of the *Firefly*," the officer answered, stepping up to Rupert and slipping a pair of handcuffs on his slender wrists. "You'd better go quietly, sir."

"Very well," Farrington answered. And then turning to me with a brave smile which wrung my heart, he said in a voice that trembled only very slightly: "Smithers, you have won our last bet. I *am* sorry—damn sorry!—that I ever read any of Martin's work!"

XIV

Weeks passed and still the crime wave swept the city. One had but to glance at the papers to see how widely this homicidal plague had spread. Other towns soon became infected. Boston, Philadelphia, and Chicago suffered even more severely than New York; and, strange to say, the police annals proved that these modern murderers sprang, not from the illiterate, uneducated classes as one might fancy, but from the reading public and more especially from the highest intellectual types.

It was during those ill-fated days that college professors, school-teachers, and literary critics began to run amuck. There was poor old Professor Brent of the university, for instance—Professor Brent who had written so many sugar-coated essays on the brotherhood of man. Who would have thought it possible that this kindly old fellow—this senile optimist whose work had always been well sweetened before it went to press—should attempt to do away with a whole class of college students one bright spring morning?

And yet one had to believe it. There it was in the papers, with a host of other incomprehensible crimes as well.

But perhaps the Southern States suffered most of all. Of late years lynching parties had been rather few and far between; now they happened again with almost machinelike regularity. Scarcely a day passed in any of those towns on the other side of the Mason and Dixon's line when some negro did not dance out his life at the end of a rope. And the leaders of these lynching parties—the men who adjusted the noose about the cowering wretch's neck or lit the fagots which had been piled up against his knees—were invariably men of keen sensibilities and higher education—men who would have shrunk from such a task a few months before.

As this crimson wave passed over the country, leaving horror and desolation in its track, the creative thinkers, who had as yet remained untouched, began to ask themselves a multitude of questions: What would be the final outcome of this catastrophe? If the higher type of intelligence fell victim to this homicidal mania, what could one expect from the illiterate, unimaginative masses who were born to follow like so many sheep? For the first time in human history, education had joined hands with crime. What would be the final dénouement? Possibly we were now facing the end of the world—a bloody end of order, a return to those primeval days when every man's hand was raised against the other.

It was during these days of dark despair, days when our modern civilization seemed tottering in the balance, that a young man gained access to the chief of the New York police force and pointed out a simple cure which had been overlooked by all the criminal experts.

Wilbur Huntington, for it was he, had some difficulty at first in securing an interview. The chief of police, on account of the many attempts made on his life, was taking no more chances with strangers. If Huntington's family had not been so prominent in the city, so influential in political circles, it is doubtful if Wilbur would have been able to gain access to that official's office. As it was, the meeting was arranged and the following conversation took place:

"Well, what can I do for you?" asked the chief, fixing a vigilant eye on his visitor.

"I came to see you about this crime wave."

"Well?"

"You want these murders stopped, don't you?" Wilbur asked simply.

For the first time in many days the chief burst out into a laugh. "Of course!" he answered.

"Well, I know how to stop them—or at least, the great majority."

Now the chief regarded his visitor with a look of fatherly pity, a look which seemed to say: "Too bad, too bad! Another madman to deal with. I'd better humor him a bit."

"It will be all right, Mr. Huntington," he said aloud. "Don't you worry your poor head about it. Just you go home and—"

But at this point, Wilbur interrupted him by stepping forward and placing a book bound in red morocco on his desk. "Here's the root of the whole matter," he declared.

"My dear young man," the chief said wearily, "I can't be bothered by this sort of thing. The State pays competent men to—"

But again Wilbur broke in upon him with scant ceremony. "I know you think I'm a crank!" he cried. "But I'm going to prove that I'm not. Will you give me five minutes of your time?"

The chief glanced at his office clock and nodded. "Fire away," said he. "Five minutes and no more."

"Students of crime know that a diseased brain often prompts murder," Huntington began quickly. "Yesterday I visited the homes of the fifty murderers who were apprehended in this city last week and in forty-five of them I found the book which I have just placed on your desk. Are you familiar with it? It is called 'The Confessions of Constantine.'"

"No," the chief answered, becoming interested in spite of himself. "But how can a book have anything to do with crime? It was merely coincidence that you found it in their homes."

"Perhaps," Huntington agreed. "But a book such as this *can* incite crime and I'm going to prove it. You, yourself, must have noticed that if an unusual murder is committed, is given publicity by the press, other murders of almost identically the same nature are sure to follow. What causes these other crimes? The answer seems obvious— mental suggestion; or, in other words, a printed description of the ghastly details which appeals to the brutal instinct in man."

"Very well put," the chief said approvingly, a note of respect creeping into his voice. "I had never thought of such a thing, but it sounds quite plausible. And you think this book could possibly—"

"I know it!" Wilbur broke in. "Just think, chief. If the description of a murder crudely written by some inartistic cub reporter can excite crime, what could not a book like 'The Confessions of Constantine' accomplish? It is a work of undoubted genius and gives one a vivid portrayal of both the murder and the sensations of bloodlust in the brain of the murderer. Why, this book can overmaster the sensitive dreamer; can hypnotize him into crime as though by the beckoning of a bloodstained finger! And here is another clew which should not be overlooked: All of these assassins are inveterate readers who live their real lives between the covers of countless books. Such people can be ruled by the printed words of a genius. A sensitive bookworm is easily excited to laughter or tears by a well-written story, so why can he not be excited to brute rage as well?"

"There is a great deal in what you say," the chief admitted. "I read quite a bit myself. Do you think this book would have any effect on me?"

"No doubt," Huntington replied. He picked up "The Confessions of Constantine" and opened it at random. "Read this short chapter," he said, handing the book to the official. "See how it affects you."

The chief, impressed in spite of himself by his guest's bizarre theory, glanced at the page Huntington indicated. Then, as Wilbur told me afterward, his attention became riveted on the book, the veins on his forehead bulged out, and a strangely sinister look crept into his eyes. Breathing heavily like a man running a race, he read page after page. At last Huntington touched him on the shoulder. Then he looked up dazedly, the whites of his eyes threaded with crimson veins.

"What is it?" he asked thickly.

But before Wilbur could answer him, the chief shook off the insidious atmosphere of the book and was himself once more. "By Heaven, you're right!" he cried, springing to his feet. "I felt like a murderer myself just now!"

"If it could affect *you* that way," Huntington said, "imagine how it would affect a nervous, high-strung man who has an enemy or a dull, brutish man who has a wrong to avenge! It seems to me that it would overthrow the brain of the one and feed the roaring beast in the other, till both would one day break through the bars of civilization!"

"You're right!" the chief repeated. "You're undoubtedly right! I can still feel the brute in me licking its lips. But what can we do? This murder propaganda is scattered all over the world by now."

"That is your problem," Huntington said, rising. "No doubt 'The Confessions of Constantine' can be traced through the Brainsworth Company and the various stores. Have the book condemned by the government, secure every copy printed, apply some kerosene and a lighted match—that's my advice. You'll soon find that, after 'The Confessions of Constantine' is done away with, this murder microbe will no longer be a menace to society. Good afternoon."

It is needless to say that his advice was taken and acted upon. Before six months had passed there were only two copies of "The Confessions of Constantine" in existence— one in Wilbur Huntington's possession, the other at police headquarters—and manslaughter had once more become a comparatively rare crime.

Indirectly Huntington's discovery saved Rupert Farrington's life. It led to a very thorough examination of the prisoners on trial for murder and a suspension of sentence when it was found that they had been mentally unbalanced by Martin's book. Rupert was transferred to

Matteawan for several months where he was under the personal supervision of several eminent brain specialists. Finally he was liberated. He returned home, thoroughly cured of his literary aspirations.

The chief of police got all the glory when the crime wave was broken, but Wilbur Huntington was allowed to keep "The Confessions of Constantine" as a souvenir.

The book soon became his evil genius.

XV

"I tell you the man is a menace to society and should be exterminated!"

It was Huntington who spoke. He had been living with me at the studio for over two weeks while his bungalow on Long Island was being renovated. Wilbur had brought "The Confessions of Constantine" with him. In spite of my protests, he had been reading portions of the condemned book aloud during the last hour and railing at the author between breaths. I did not like his air of unusual excitement and sought to calm him.

"Martin could hardly have guessed that his work would cause so much suffering and crime," I ventured.

"He couldn't, eh?" Huntington cried. "Well, I think he could. In fact, I'm sure of it. A genius never underestimates his work. I believe he knew exactly what effect 'The Confessions of Constantine' would have on the reading public."

"Oh, come now, Wilbur! That's a little bit too much!"

"I believe he planned it!" Huntington continued stubbornly. "Any man who could formulate in his brain such terrible thoughts and who had such a brutally vivid imagination, would delight in the results. Each murder would seem like a new leaf in his crown of victory; they would whisper in his ear that he, alone, was master of his art. I can fairly see him chuckling over the gruesome headlines of the papers, can fairly hear him saying to himself, 'This—all this—is *my* work!'"

He paused for breath. His heightened color and flashing eyes once more indicated an unhealthy excitement entirely foreign to the man. Again I sought to calm him.

"I don't like Martin any better than you do, Wilbur. But I think you do him an injustice in this. You just alluded to his brutally vivid imagination. Well, the truth is that he has no imagination at all. He clearly told me as much when we were in Paris together. No doubt he gets his themes secondhand, from the riffraff he associates with."

"No imagination?" Huntington muttered. "No imagination?"

"No, not a grain of it—or so he says. He told me that he had a remarkable memory which served him as well."

"That's strange! Then how does he describe so vividly what is taking place in the murderer's brain? 'The Confessions of Constantine' is brimming over with the psychological sensations of the assassin."

"No doubt he knows many murderers," I answered. "Possibly they confide in him."

Huntington threw back his head and laughed. "The sensations of an assassin must be difficult to describe," he said at length. "The ordinary criminal could not express them. Have you ever been in love, Charley?"

"In a very mild way, perhaps."'

"Well, let me hear you describe the sensations of love."

I hesitated for a minute. "I don't believe I can do it," I said. "At least, not clearly. I felt very happy and that sort of thing."

"Of course, you can't describe them. It takes genius to portray vividly any of the great passions. Hate is just as difficult as love. Martin *can* portray hate. You say he does it without imagination—that means without the knack of climbing into any one else's skin. Are you sure that he told you he had no imagination, Charley?"

"Quite sure. I remember distinctly everything he said."

Wilbur closed his eyes, and, interlacing his pudgy fingers over his paunch, sank back on the lounge. Such an attitude of abandon meant that he was thinking deeply. It was quite characteristic of the man to sink into a kind of coma and then come to the surface again grasping an illusive fact. As I sat watching his recumbent figure, I was prepared for some startling manifestation of uncanny insight.

At last Huntington sat up and rubbed his eyes. "Have you got Martin's first book about the premises?" he asked.

"'Many Murders'? Yes. Do you want to see it?"

"Yes, indeed, Charley," he murmured. "Perhaps we can read between the lines."

I took "Many Murders" out of the bookcase and handed it to him. He opened it at random and read a portion of "In a Blind Alley" aloud. At length he closed the book and picked up "The Confessions of Constantine."

"He didn't have to have imagination to write *that* story, Charley," he said. "You shared the adventure with him, I believe?"

"Yes, it was that murder in the alley I told you about. He saw it all."

Huntington nodded and opened "The Confessions, of Constantine." For some time he read silently, moving his lips. He seemed to be weighing each word. Finally he spoke again.

"'Many Murders' came out before your brother's death, didn't it?" he asked.

"Yes."

"And 'The Confessions of Constantine' about two years after his death?"

"I believe so."

"Then I have a little theory which, if it stands the acid test of truth, will put Martin *hors de combat* for good and all. Perhaps the world has little more to fear from him."

"I'm sure I don't know what you're driving at, Wilbur."

"Have patience, Charley. Listen! I think I hear some one tapping on your door."

When I flung the door open, I found a freckled messenger boy in the corridor. He had a registered letter for Wilbur, addressed in very small but legible writing—writing which, for some unaccountable reason, seemed familiar. Signing for the letter, I returned to Huntington.

"Here's a letter for you," I said, handing him the note. "Whoever addressed this envelope has a confoundedly steady hand. It's like engraving."

"You're an inquisitive cuss!" Huntington murmured. "Perhaps it's from a lady friend."

He tore open the envelope and glanced at its contents. The next moment, his eyebrows crawled up his forehead in surprise. "Speaking about the devil!" he cried. "Well, what do you know about this!"

"Nothing. But I'd like to. That handwriting interests me. There's something familiar about it. Is it from your mother?"

"Not exactly!" Huntington replied. "Just listen to this." Holding the letter on a level with his eyes, he began to read as follows:

My Dear Mr. Huntington: I understand that you have recently become a literary critic. Allow me to congratulate you on your judgment in regard to my book, 'The Confessions of Constantine.' No doubt, as you so wisely pointed out to the police, it was a work which proved rather detrimental to the morals of the reading public. By condemning it, the government paid me the highest tribute which can fall to the lot of any artist—the tribute of taking my mental creations seriously.

I have just finished another book of short stories, and I should like your opinion of it before it goes to press. As you have constituted yourself a moral censor, a Mother Grundy of literature, I feel obliged to be guided by your advice. Will you do me the honor of calling at eight o'clock tonight?

Very sincerely,

Burgess Martin

"You evidently have him worried," I said. "Are you going?"

Huntington paused for a moment before he answered. Finally he raised his eyes to my face and I saw that they were flashing like slits in a furnace door.

"Yes, I'm going!" he cried. "This time I see my way clear. I'll strike him down, Charley; I'll put my foot on his neck! Perhaps I can suggest a new idea for his book—something that even *he* has never thought of. He has described crime from the standpoint of the spectator, from the standpoint of the criminal; but are there not other lengths to which he could go? Martin's mind must be like an overladen camel. One more straw, and then—But we'll see, Charley; we'll see."

Huntington rose to his feet with the intention of leaving the apartment. I was in a bewildered state as I followed him to the door. My friend's incomprehensible words made me fear for his reason. Was it possible that "The Confessions of Constantine" was conquering his mind as it had conquered Rupert Farrington's?

"When will you be back?" I asked as he slipped on his coat.

"Not for two days. I promised my mother to visit her for a while." He took my hand in leave-taking and pressed it warmly. "We've been good friends, you and I," he said with one of his rare smiles. "We've had lots of fun together. That's pleasant to think over, isn't it? Good night, Charley."

What could have come over Huntington, I wondered as the door closed behind him. Something had changed him utterly. He, the most undemonstrative of men, had actually held my hand like a lovesick schoolgirl. He had said good-bye to me as though we were parting for years instead of for days. What could it all mean?

XVI

A week passed and I saw nothing of Huntington. This was strange, to say the least, as he had promised to look me up in a day or so and let me know how his interview with Martin had turned out. Vague misgivings began to torment me as I remembered his rather bewildering statements in regard to "The Confessions of Constantine." Had the book thrown him off his mental balance as it had Rupert Farrington, Professor Brent, and so many others?

On the following Tuesday Mrs. Huntington phoned me. No sooner did I hear her high, fretful voice than I had a premonition of disaster.

"Yes, Mrs. Huntington," I answered. "This is Mr. Smithers. What can I do for you this morning?"

"You might send Wilbur home. I haven't seen him in months."

"Send Wilbur home?" I repeated dazedly. "Why, he left here last week, Mrs. Huntington! He told me then that he intended staying with you the rest of the time he was in New York."

There came a long-drawn silence and then a deafening volley of words. "Why, he never came! I haven't seen him for over two months. Do you suppose anything could have happened to the poor boy? Oh, I'm so frightened! He was such a reckless driver! He might have driven his car out into the country and had a smash-up on some lonely road. What shall I do, Mr. Smithers?"

"Please be calm," I told her. "No doubt Wilbur is all right. Probably he's gone out to Long Island. Have you called up his bungalow?"

"No, of course not! I thought he was with you."

"Well, phone there and I'm pretty sure you'll find him. If not, call me up. I'll find him for you."

"Thank you so much! Probably you're right. But he should have let me know. Good-by, Mr. Smithers."

"Good-by," I answered and hung up the receiver with a feeling of uncertainty.

For the rest of that morning I attempted to paint, but made a miserable failure of it. Try as I would, I could not fix my attention on the work at hand. Huntington's incomprehensible words about Martin kept ringing through my head. At last I tossed the brush aside and left the studio with the intention of inquiring for Wilbur at the Cap and Gown Club.

I was descending the stairs and had reached the first landing when I came face to face with a small man who was coming up. I was about to stand aside so as to give him room to pass, when he addressed me.

"Are you Mr. Smithers?" he asked.

"Yes," I said in surprise. "What can I do for you?"

"I want to ask you a few questions about a friend of yours. You know Wilbur Huntington, I presume?"

"Yes, indeed."

"Well, I think we'd better have our talk in your apartment, if you don't mind."

I led the way back to the studio with the feeling that something quite unexpected was about to happen. In fact, my brain was in a whirl. Who could this rather common-looking little man be? And what could he possibly want to know about Huntington?

But my visitor gave me no time to compose myself. No sooner had the door closed behind us than he spoke.

"I understand that Mr. Huntington was here on the afternoon of the twenty-fifth?"

"Yes, he was."

"I'm Greene from police headquarters," the little man continued, opening his coat and displaying a metal badge. "As I believe you know, Mr. Huntington has been missing now for several days. His mother has just put the case in our hands."

"He wasn't at his bungalow, then?"

"No, he hasn't been there in over a month. Mrs. Huntington thought you might be able to give us valuable information. Where was he going when he left your apartment, Mr. Smithers?"

"He was going to the house of Mr. Burgess Martin on Tyndall Place."

"Burgess Martin, eh? That's interesting! Was there anything unusual about Mr. Huntington's manner— anything which would lead you to suspect that he wasn't in a normal state of mind?"

Then I did a very foolish thing—a thing which I have regretted ever since. I revealed everything to the detective, answering his questions with the candor of a child. I told him of the letter Huntington had received, of his wild words about Martin, and of his final threat. And when I had finished, my visitor thanked me heartily.

"If other people were as willing to give evidence as you, Mr. Smithers," said he, "the work of a detective would soon dwindle down to nothing. What you say about Burgess Martin is especially interesting. Word has just come to us that he, too, is missing."

"What?"

"Yes, his landlady hasn't seen him in days." The detective turned toward the door. "I've got to be off on this new clew you've given me, Mr. Smithers," he called back over his shoulder. "It's just possible, if we can lay our hands on Mr. Huntington, that he'll be able to tell us something about Burgess Martin."

When the detective had gone, I realized fully what I had done. I had branded my best friend as a murderer. I had slipped the halter about his neck. Then, for the first time, I saw clearly the significance of Wilbur's threatening words when coupled with the disappearance of Martin. Yes, I had made an ass of myself. But there was no helping that now. The damage was done. I could do nothing more—only wait as patiently as possible for the results.

Days turned into weeks, weeks into months, but the two men still remained missing. Meanwhile the newspapers made much of the mystery and soon it became the sensation of the year. It was remembered that it was through Wilbur Huntington's efforts that Martin's last book had been condemned by the government. From that fact, they argued that there was bad blood between the two men, and this gave rise to all manner of wild conjectures. Possibly they had fought a duel to the death; or perhaps it had a suicide pact. The yellow journals knew how to make hay while the sun shone.

Nearly two months after the detective visited me, a body was found floating in the East River. The face had been beaten into an unrecognizable condition by some heavy weapon and the corpse generally was so disfigured by its long submersion in the water, that, had it not been for a ring on the second finger of the left hand, identification would have proved impossible. This ring was engraved with the initials B. M.

The news spread quickly through the city. Newspaper extras appeared with startling headlines. For a time excitement quickened the most feeble pulse. On all sides, one heard this question—"But where is Wilbur Huntington?"

On the following day the rumor was verified. Martin's tailor, a little Russian Jew who had made his clothes for many years, visited the morgue and identified the corpse's water-soaked suit by his own initials which he had sewed into the sleeve. After this there could no longer be any doubt; it was indeed Burgess Martin's body.

But if Martin had been murdered, as the wounds on his face and head evinced, what had become of his companion, Wilbur Huntington, on the night when they had both disappeared? Had Huntington killed Martin and then fled? If he were innocent, would he not come forward and prove it?

Questions like these appeared in all the papers. But the missing man still remained missing; the mystery was no nearer its solution than before. No doubt the chief of police at this time was pestered daily by hundreds of letters from cranks who had worked themselves up into a frenzy over this insoluble riddle. At last he wrote an article for the *Gazette* which ended in these words:

> It is not possible that Wilbur Huntington, after saving the world from a thousand crimes, failed to take his own cure and fell a victim to that brain malady from which he had rescued so many others!

After this opinion was published, there could be but one verdict. The world regarded my friend as a murderer and a madman.

XVII

Several years passed and the mystery still remained unsolved. It was as though Wilbur Huntington had vanished into thin air. Although many of the leading criminal experts had taken up the search, no clew to his whereabouts was forthcoming. One by one these detectives acknowledged themselves beaten and went back to the solving of less difficult problems. Meanwhile new sensational mysteries a rose to attract the attention of the public; soon the affair was practically forgotten.

During that time, I prospered exceedingly. Each year brought me greater wealth, a larger circle of acquaintances, and more material luxuries of every kind. I had won the respect of a great many people who envied me my position in the world—people who little guessed what had sacrificed in order to climb.

I soon learned that the respect of the mob was of small value. The world, as a whole, judges an artist as it judges a business man—not by the excellence of his work, but by the size of his bank account. I was a symbol to them of the golden image and they prostrated themselves accordingly. Little guessing the bitter irony their words conveyed, they called me to my face "the painter who had made good." Sometimes it gave me a kind of brutal satisfaction to realize how completely I had sold the public. But now and then another thought would steal into my brain—the thought that I had not sold the public but had, in reality, sold myself. On these occasions, I was far from a happy man.

Ten years after Wilbur Huntington's disappearance, I laid my brush aside for the last time. I was now forty and had amassed a comfortable fortune. It seemed to me that I had earned the right to play. But those years of drudgery at the easel had taken away all youthful buoyancy. My health was not what it should have been. I consulted a physician and he advised me to take a vacation in the wilds of Florida.

"Why not come along with me to Naples?" Dr. Street suggested. "I'm going to make the trip, as usual, on the fifteenth. You'll want some one with you who knows the ropes."

I agreed to his proposition with pleasure. I had known him long enough to realize that he would make an excellent camping companion. But, unfortunately for our plans, when the day arrived Doctor Street was detained in New York much against his will. As all my preparations were made, I decided not to wait for him. He was careful to point out the exact locality of the hotel where I should meet him a week later.

"By the way," he said as we parted, "don't forget to hire Bill Pete when you get to the hotel. He's the best guide in all Florida. Make him take you over to his hut on the other side of the bay and give you some fishing. What you need is exercise and fresh air."

The trip to Florida was uneventful. I got off the train at Fort Myers and engaged a dilapidated Ford to take me to Naples. The driver gave me a hand with my numerous belongings, climbed back on his seat, and we were off.

It was a forty mile drive from Fort Myers over a road sadly needing repair. Two hours later I caught sight of the wooden structure which my driver assured me was the hotel In spite of my natural fatigue, I warmed to the majestic scene which had appeared with the startling suddenness of a vision.

There, stretching away as far as the eye could see, was the Gulf of Mexico, now reflecting on its slightly agitated bosom the last scattered rays of the setting sun. Already the dark shadows of approaching night stole out from the palm trees which lined the beach. The melancholy call of an owl suddenly rose on the still air and was thrown to and fro by a multitude of echoes before it was allowed to die away.

Naples was known to only a limited number of sportsmen. There were not more than a dozen people at the hotel when I arrived. I felt fairly certain that I could secure the services of Bill Pete. After dinner I inquired about him at the desk.

"No, he's not here now," the clerk informed me. "But he generally paddles over for his newspaper about eight o'clock. I'll let you know when he arrives."

I nodded and, lighting a cigar, strolled out on the veranda. The moon, by now, was slowly rising over the treetops—a blood-red moon which, as it ascended, gradually lost its vivid coloring and became a pale silver. Under its magic touch, the surface of the water was transformed into a sea of drifting sparks. The wind had risen. Now and then the crest of a wave was illumined, becoming for an instant a curling, foamflecked lip. It was a night of ebony and silver.

"How beautiful it is," I murmured half-aloud.

"It may be beautiful," said a voice at my elbow, "but it is horrible as well!"

I started, for I had thought myself alone. Now I could see the tall, dark figure of a man leaning against the railing of the veranda within arm's reach of me. How was it that I had not heard his footsteps? He had not been there a moment before; of that I was certain.

"Horrible?" I repeated slowly. "Why is it horrible?"

"Look!" he cried, pointing at the sky with a dramatic gesture. "What do you see? That is no smile on the moon's face, although there are fools who think it is. No, it is a grimace of despair like one sees on a death's head when the jaw drops down. And how white she is, how ghastly white! True, the moon has a round face; but it is the more terrible for that. She has the bloated look of decomposing flesh. And what have become of her eyes? Have the vultures picked out her eyes?"

I moved my feet uneasily. What an unpleasant imagination this fellow had! How could people turn such a beautiful night into a charnel house? Probably this man was some crackbrained poet or other. There was something familiar about his voice—something which I could not account for and which irritated me.

"It is though Nature had placed that death's-head in the heavens as a warning to all mankind," he continued solemnly. "Oh perhaps She hung it there to kindle the imagination, to beckon us on to unparalleled achievement, to blow into flame a glowing spark of curiosity. What is death and what are the sensations of death? Who can answer? And yet mankind is unwilling to learn. They hide the truth from themselves, disguising it under many different masks. They play with the moon as a baby might play with the face of its dead mother. They even write songs about her, calling her the jolly, smiling moon! And all these years that great white face has looked down upon them in frozen horror!"

I felt the mental itch of curiosity as I listened. Where had I heard that voice before? He had been speaking in a very low tone, but each word had a familiar ring.

"I think I must have met you before," I said. "You're a poet, aren't you? I used to know a good many poets when I lived in Washington Square."

"I am no poet," he said curtly.

"But you write," I insisted. "I'm sure I've heard your voice before. I used to know several novelists. There was—"

"I don't write," he broke in rather brusquely. "My name's Bill Pete and I've lived around here nearly all my life."

"Not Bill Pete, the guide?" I cried in amazement.

"The very same. The clerk told me that you were looking for me. If you want a guide, I think you'll find that I know my business. I'm familiar with every rookery in these parts and I've got a snug little cabin across the bay if you were thinking of camping out."

"So you're Bill Pete," I muttered under my breath.

"Well, you've got a most astonishing vocabulary for a backwoodsman!" Aloud, I said: "You've worked for Doctor Street?"

"Yes, frequently. He always engages me when he comes to the hotel."

"Then, you're the man I want. You may consider yourself engaged from now on. I think I'll use your cabin to-morrow night. Is it comfortable?"

"Yes, sir," Bill Pete murmured. "I think you'll find it very comfortable."

Once more I shot a quick look at that tall, shadowy figure beside me. I *had* heard him speak before; each moment I grew surer of it. When was it and where? I would find out in the course of the next two or three days—that was certain.

"You'll pardon me if ask a rather personal question, Mr. Pete?" I said. "You didn't your education in the woods, did you? Your choice of words seems to be rather fine, rather—"

I broke off suddenly. A moonbeam had touched the side of his face. I could see that his heavily bearded cheeks and chin were trembling as though from suppressed merriment, and yet his voice was quite steady when he answered me.

"I'm a college man, sir," he replied, moving his head slightly so that his face was once more veiled in shadow. "I've had my chances and I've thrown them away. There are lots of us like that." He paused for an instant and then added: "Good night, sir. I'll paddle over for you in the morning."

XVIII

The following morning, Bill Pete paddled me across
the bay to his cabin with the deft, silent strokes of an
Indian. Sitting in the bow of the canoe and facing him, I
studied the man, attempting to account for the impression I
had had the night before. But, try as I would, my memory
failed me.

Certainly there was nothing familiar in that bronzed,
heavily bearded face. And yet there was something about
Bill Pete which struck a long disused, discordant note in
my breast. What was it? His eyes? They were hidden behind
dark-blue spectacles which resembled the cavernous sockets
in a skull. Perhaps the answer to the riddle was concealed
by these spectacles. For one mad moment I was tempted to
spring forward and jerk them off his nose.

"Why do you wear those things?" I said at length.

"What things?" he asked blankly. Although his face
was half turned away from me, I felt instinctively that his
eyes were boring into mine.

"Why, those spectacles," I said testily. "They make your face look like a skull."

"My eyes are very weak. These glasses protect them from the sun."

"Oh, I see."

Not another word was said till the canoe grounded on the beach. I assisted Bill Pete in moving the provisions we had brought with us into the shade; then he showed me his cabin.

It was an ordinary woodsman's shack, built of roughhewn logs and containing two bunks. There was a crudely constructed table in the center of the single room, some pots and pans hanging on the wall, a wood stove in one corner, and a doorway without any vestige of a door. To a city-bred man, no building is complete without a door. This architectural omission bothered me till I learned that no wild animal availed itself of it with the single exception of a razor-back hog that each night entered after we had gone to bed and gnawed savagely at one of the logs.

Barely a hundred yards from the cabin, which stood on a slight rise of ground, the bay stretched out like a luminous shawl of bright spangles. Encircling it, was a dark somber army of tropical trees which stood like sentinels about a treasure. On windy nights, the lapping waves on the beach and the murmuring of the branches overhead mingled in a soothing melody which soon wafted one off to the land of dreams.

Bill Pete proved to be a very silent man, speaking very rarely and then always to the point. A smile seldom brightened his somber face. But although he was a poor companion, he proved to be an excellent guide. He knew the woods like the creatures of the woods; his tread was so noiseless that he could creep up to within a few feet of a feeding deer before the animal sprang away in fright; and he knew with unfaltering intuition where the largest tarpon glided. Under his guidance, I had some excellent fishing.

This healthy, outdoor life worked wonders with my shattered nerves. The long tramps through the woods, the invigorating air, the nights of unbroken repose, were fast making a new man of me. Before the week had passed I felt an entirely different individual from the broken-down portrait painter who had left New York under the doctor's orders. It is no telling how healthy I would have become, had it not been for that night of unparalleled horror through which I passed—that night when I saw a black soul stripped bare and writhing out its life alone.

It had been a hard day's tramp through the forest. I felt deliciously tired as I lay before the log fire. Bill Pete sat a few feet from me. His corncob pipe was gripped between his teeth; his face, as usual, was veiled in shadow. The wind had been rising steadily for upward of an hour; now and then I could hear the rumble of thunder far off. Our fire would spring up fiercely at each eddying gust; and, as the bright curling fingers of flame grasped at the upper darkness, the encircling tree trunks would seem to take a long stride forward and then leap back again.

"It looks as though we were going to have a stormy night," I said at length.

Bill Pete nodded and puffed silver rings of smoke skyward. His spectacles for an instant reflected the firelight as he turned his face toward me.

"Doctor Street will be here to-morrow," I continued in a desperate attempt to make the man talk. "You'd better paddle over to the hotel in the morning."

Again Bill Pete merely nodded his head.

"You remind me of a man I used to know a good many years ago," I said irritably. "Like you, he had unpleasant theories about the moon and for days together would scarcely say a word."

"Who was he?" Bill Pete asked, with a sudden note of interest in his tone.

"A man by the name of Martin—Burgess Martin."

I heard something snap like a dry twig. Glancing at Bill Pete, I saw the red glowing bowl of his pipe lying on the ground at his feet. He had bitten through the stem.

"And what became of Burgess Martin?" he asked after a moment.

"Why, you must know!" I said in surprise. "He was that famous writer who was murdered several years ago. Surely you remember the case?"

"I believe I did read something about it," he answered in a low voice. "He was murdered by a literary critic, wasn't he? The murderer's name was Huntington, I believe; and he had previously had one of Martin's books condemned by the government."

"That's never been proved," I said with some heat. "Wilbur Huntington was a personal friend of mine and one of the finest fellows in the world. If he *did* kill Martin, it was because he was mentally deranged at the time."

Bill Pete burst out into an unpleasant laugh. "Why do the masses believe that a murderer must be insane?" he cried. "Surely to kill is the natural instinct of man. You say that Huntington was a fine fellow. Well, what has that got to do with it? How can any one gain the fineness and fullness of living without first feasting on the lives of others?"

"I disagree with you," I said with a yawn; "but I'm too tired to argue. I think I'll turn in."

"Don't let me keep you up," he muttered.

I took a last look at the shadows which played under the trees and entered the cabin. As I moved about, getting ready for bed, I could see Bill Pete's dark figure silhouetted against the firelight. Like a carved idol of wood, he sat perfectly motionless.

It did not take me long to fall asleep that night. Hardly had I crawled between the blankets and closed my eyes, before I was swept far out on the sea of dreams. And in these dreams, I was conscious of something which was approaching steadily and relentlessly—something which threatened my very existence. I felt that I must escape. I tried to struggle but I was held down by bands of steel. Nearer and nearer that relentless presence approached. Now I could feel its warm breath on my cheek.

I awoke, bathed in perspiration, to a sensation of supernatural dread. The oil lamp on the table was lit. I could see every object distinctly. There, with his back toward me, stood Bill Pete. What was he doing at this hour of the night? Why, he was shaving! He was standing before the small mirror I had hung on the wall and was shaving! He held one of my razors; I could see the blade glimmer faintly as he lowered his arm for an instant.

Still in a mental daze of sleep, I stared at his back. Then I glanced at the shaving glass. What I saw there, will live in my memory always. I tried to rise, but I could not; I tried to cry out, but my tongue clove to the roof of my mouth.

"Who are you?" I gasped.

And now the tall figure was turning toward me. I saw that well-remembered face, thin, ascetic, with lips that curled upward like a cat's; I saw those cold, gray eyes which held in their depths a speculative stare; I saw the man, himself, approaching with a stealthy, noiseless tread. The mirror had not lied. It was Burgess Martin!

XIX

There is no fear which man can experience so gripping, so subduing, as fear of the supernatural. When the mind cannot explain, when all the rivers of thought are frozen at their source, we become children again in the imagination, children who people the dark with living phantoms. Life is then no longer the familiar highway, brightly lighted, with the kindly signposts of convention at every crossing, but a shadowy cave of horrors through which we must grope blindly. What lies waiting for us in the gloom? We do not know, we cannot guess—and therein lies the fear. Such a sensation is indeed terrible.

Here, in this dimly lighted cabin, far from all the reassuring realities of life, I was looking into the face of a man whom I had every reason to believe dead and buried years ago! Was it any wonder that I could neither move nor cry out, that I stared silently at this apparition like a terror-stricken child?

Although my brain was spinning dizzily like a top, although Burgess Martin's steadfast eyes held mine like magnets, I was instinctively aware of the objects immediately surrounding me. For instance, I knew that a blanket had been fastened securely across the doorway to keep out the wind which now howled in baffled fury about the cabin; and yet I had not even glanced in that direction.

The long-threatening storm had risen. Now the first drops of rain were pattering on the roof like tiny fingers tapping for admittance. Suddenly there came a blinding flash of lightning, followed almost immediately by a deafening peal of thunder. Again there was silence. Nature seemed to hold her breath.

"Why do you fear me, Smithers?" said a voice which I knew only too well. "I am no ghost."

By now Burgess Martin was standing beside my bunk, looking down on me with a gleam of derision in his eyes. Mustering all my courage, I attempted to sit up. Then, for the first time, I realized that I was tied hand and foot with strong leather straps which a giant could scarcely have broken.

"It is useless to struggle, Smithers," Martin continued coldly; "not only useless but dangerous. My patience is worn thin. When I think of what I have suffered, when I think of what art has suffered, I can have no more tolerance for stupidity."

"Then you weren't murdered after all?" I muttered through dry lips.

"Most assuredly not," he answered with one of his catlike grimaces. Seating himself on the side of the bunk, he regarded me with a speculative stare. "Why is man invariably blinded by the obvious?" he continued. "A chain of circumstantial evidence can so easily be forged by a master mind that one should test it thoroughly before one believes. Why should you think that Wilbur Huntington murdered me?"

"I never thought so," I muttered.

"Ah, but you did, Smithers," he said lifting one of his long, thin hands in expostulation. "*You* did and the world did. And why? Simply because a body was found floating in the East River—a decomposing, unrecognizable body which wore my ring and clothes. And because *he* visited me that night, because he disliked my works, because he disappeared—you, his best friend, branded him a murderer. What a trifling thing I renounced when I sacrificed friendship on the altar!"

He paused as another reverberating peal of thunder shook the cabin. For an instant his sallow face was illumined by a sickly flash of lightning; I saw a tiny, pendulous drop of blood on his chin where the razor had slipped and nicked the flesh. Strange to say, the sight of this single crimson bead of blood was reassuring; it spurred my flagging courage. If he could bleed, surely he was human.

"And what became of Wilbur Huntington?" I asked.

"Why, it was *his* body which was floating down the river," Martin answered coldly. "He wore my clothes and ring, and the water had changed him somewhat—that was all."

Once more horror overmastered me. I caught a glimpse of the truth "Who murdered him?" I cried. "Good God, Martin, did you—"

He bowed and I saw a smile crease his cheek like a scar. "Of course, Smithers. Wasn't it the natural outcome of his visit to me that night? This man stood in my path—in the path of art. I had to destroy him, or else my ambition was doomed. He had become an insurmountable obstacle in my path. I could go no further until I had forcibly removed him. How simple, how true! Why, even *he* had a premonition of the truth. He came to my rooms as a hero goes to battle. He was a brave man, Smithers."

Once more Martin paused and stroked his chin. I saw the pendulous drop of blood stain his finger tips. And now this blood was no longer reassuring. It revolted me. Those vibrating crimson finger tips were a symbol—a symbol of the stealthy assassin who slays by night. Soon they might be fastened about my throat—or, perhaps, they would grasp the hilt of the hunting knife suspended from his belt. No matter how death came, those finger tips would play their part in it.

I felt that life and I were soon to part. Like a fallen tree trunk, I was at the mercy of this forester of lives. He confided in me so readily because he judged me as one already dead. It amused him to play on my emotions before he cut the thin thread which held me to existence. He was confessing to me now as a cat might confess to the mouse between its paws.

But I would keep a stiff upper lip! I was afraid— yes, deadly afraid—but he should never know it. He had laughed at me many times. He had called me a weakling. He had held me up to ridicule. But I would show him that I could face death. Perhaps I did not have the courage to brave life, but I had the courage to brave death. I would show him *that*—I would show him that even a weakling knew how to die.

"Why did you tie me?" I asked at length. "Are you going to murder me?'

He started and glanced up. "Not necessarily. Perhaps you will want to go. Man lives to learn; why cannot he die to learn? Is it not strange that human curiosity cannot overcome human fear? Are you afraid of the dark, Smithers? Will you not open the door for truth? What is the exact sensation of death, Smithers? Tell me—has that question never worried you?"

"Never," I muttered. "Why should it?"

Martin shrugged his shoulders. "Perhaps it shouldn't. But to me, it—well, you wouldn't understand. Only the moon understands. But you must listen to my story. No doubt you will think it one long, red road of wanton cruelty and mad blood lust. No doubt you will be unable to appreciate the supreme sacrifice of a strong nature—the sacrifice of human flesh, of human love, on the altar of the muse—that sacrifice to kindle the immortal flame of genius and create the indestructible. What *I* have done for art no man has done; what *I* will do for art you must bear witness to. I have chosen you as my messenger to the world."

At that instant a shaft of lightning flashed between us like a lifted sword blade. It was immediately followed by such a deafening peal of thunder that the tiny cabin echoed it like a hollow drum. Now the rain came down in a silver deluge, tapping on the boards overhead as though a multitude of hammers were at work. Several drops trickled through a chink between the logs and fell on my upturned face. And they kept on falling relentlessly while I listened to Martin's confession.

XX

"As you already know, Smithers," Martin began, "my parents both died when I was very young and my aunt took me to live with her. In that great, gloomy house the books were my only companion. And what a collection! I believe every great horror tale ever written found a permanent resting place on the shelves which circled her library. And beside these, there were scores of volumes dealing with spiritualism and necromancy—volumes, gray with the dust of centuries, between whose covers lay many a forgotten tragedy like vivid, crimson flowers. And how I loved them all! How I lingered over them, forgetting time and place, drinking in great drafts of knowledge, reading on and on till often the pallid face of morning peered in at me through my window!

"But soon ambition began to lash me. Why could I not create horror tales which in no way would be inferior to those I now devoured with such avidity? Perhaps I might write even better. Certainly I had the will to persevere.

No one could be more painstaking, no one could be more thorough. Surely, if Carlyle were right in his definition of genius, I might aspire to any heights.

"Thinking thus, I sat down in the library one sunny afternoon to start my career as a short-story writer, to create my first horror tale. Gradually, as the minutes passed, bright optimism flickered like the flame of a candle one breathes upon. I had thought that inspiration would envelop me like a fiery mantle, that I would be lifted out of myself and home away to some strange kingdom of fancy where I could pick and choose from an unlimited treasure. But nothing of the kind happened. On the contrary, my mind seemed a vacuum. And then realized the sickening truth: I was attempting to write and had no imagination!

"Then I suffered, Smithers, as only the very young can suffer. Ambition was already planted deep in my soul and I felt that it could never flower without imagination. Tears gushed from my eyes; I was a plaything for grief. No doubt my literary career would have ended there and then, had it not been for the strange occurrence which befell on that same, sunshiny afternoon.

"My aunt had been very sick for over a month. Now she was dying. As I sat with weak tears running down my face, her nurse entered the library and took me to the sick room to say a last farewell. No doubt she considered that my emotion was caused by natural grief at the expectation of losing a near relative. She wiped my eyes and attempted to console me, before she led me to my aunt's bedside.

"The old lady was almost at her last gasp. Her thin, yellow hands were fluttering over the coverlet, resembling the fallen, windswept leaves of autumn; the death rattle rasped harshly in her wizened throat with the mechanical vibration of an engine running down; her heavy, blue-veined eyelids were closed and did not open as I knelt beside her. Soon her breathing stopped. She was dead.

"On my way back to the library, the scene which I had just witnessed was pictured in glowing colors in my brain. Nothing could wipe it out. Wherever I looked, I saw my aunt lying in her great four-poster bed like a fallen branch on a snowbank.

"Once more I picked up my discarded paper and pencil and began idly to picture in words what I had just seen. And then a strange thing happened. I seemed to be again in the sick room which I had just quitted—alone there with the dying woman, listening to her wheezing breath and watching her dry, shriveled hands fluttering about like autumn leaves circling in the wind.

"How long this strange mental hallucination possessed me, I do not know. When I regained normal consciousness, it was to find both sides of the paper covered with my microscopic writing. With amazement, I read aloud what I had written.

"You cannot imagine my feelings, Smithers, when I realized that what I was reading was a masterpiece of description. As clear-cut and convincing as an ivory carving, it had a vividness of detail, a charm of style, which held the attention in an iron grip. To be sure, it was merely a sketch—a word-painting of my aunt's death—but, for all that, it was worthy of immortality.

"And there could be no mistake—*I* had composed this morbid masterpiece. It was my writing without a doubt. What did it matter that I had been unconscious of the manual effort which guided the pencil? Surely true inspiration lifted the artist out of the shell in which he lived his normal days. And yet *was* this true inspiration? Surely not. This was no flight of the imagination. It was a realistic description of something I had seen with my own eyes and heard with my own ears. My aunt's death had been photographed on the film of my brain and I had developed it with all the art of a stylist into this perfect picture.

"Now true realization of the truth was born in upon me. I was, indeed, a writer without imagination and therefore I must rely solely on what I saw with my own eyes and what I heard with my own ears. I had determined to devote myself to horror tales. Very well. But in order to be a master of tragedy, I must steel my heart against all weakness, all feeling; I must, perhaps, witness the perpetration of crime so as to impress my readers with its reality. It was necessary for an unimaginative artist to associate with the scum of the world in order to rise above the world. Therefore I must tear out my heart so that my head might rise above the stars. All this I realized, but I did not turn back."

There came another crash of thunder which drowned him out. His next few words were lost, swallowed up by the rattling of the pots and pans on the wall, the tapping fingers of rain, and a gust of wind which went howling about the cabin.

"For many months I trained myself for my future career," Martin resumed. "Fortunately, at that time, I had no friends except a few household pets on which I had centered my affections. Because I loved them, I knew that they must go. I must have no human weaknesses to hold me back—nothing which could later interfere with art by making my will subordinate to mercy.

"So, coldly, methodically, but with unparalleled mental anguish, I tortured to death each one of my poor pets.

My brain reeled, but my hand was steady; and, after each atrocious act, I felt the natural repulsion for these cruelties growing less and less. I slowly conquered myself.

"It was about this time that I first took up drawing with the intention of illustrating my future work. As in writing, it came naturally to me when death was my model. Sitting before one of my slaughtered pets, I would first write a vivid description of its demise and then draw a striking, realistic picture of the scene. I kept a child's diary, illustrated with no little skill, depicting the various crimes I had committed and portraying my various emotions with such clarity of vision that I am sure it would have had a disastrous effect on the minds of other children had it been published. Like 'The Confessions of Constantine,' it might have created a wave of crime

"Shortly after this, I entered a nearby school and almost immediately obtained the theme for my first short story. One afternoon, while walking home, I saw one of my classmates—a rather pretty girl whom I had unconsciously grown quite fond of—on the arm of an overgrown yokel whose vacant eyes and moving lips indicated a weak mentality. That evening I made inquiries in town and discovered that this yokel often carried her books home from school and that she tolerated him only out of kindness. It was plain to see that he adored her and that he was extremely jealous as are most weak-minded persons.

"On the following day, I won the affections of the poor fellow by some small kindness and ascertained that my theory was correct. His brain was like a clouded mirror, but he loved the girl devotedly. You know the rest, Smithers. I wrote it up in 'The Murder of Mary Mortimer.'

"I was the voice which drove the poor idiot on, the voice who turned the love in his undeveloped nature into a seething inferno of jealous hatred. And then, when he murdered her, when I saw her fall bleeding on a carpet of soft white snow, I stole out of the bushes where I had concealed myself and made a sketch of her. You remember the painting, I think. It was a vivid portrayal, but rather crude in its color scheme."

Martin broke off and regarded me intently. Seeing the horror written on my face, no doubt, he attempted to explain and thereby made his crime all the more revolting.

"To say that I felt no compassion for her would be to lie," he continued. "As I told you, Smithers, I was fond of the girl—dangerously fond. Otherwise I would not have driven the idiot to kill her. A dozen times I was on the point of leaping forward, of rescuing her before it was too late; and a dozen times the voice of reason whispered: 'Fool, fool, would you refuse art your first human sacrifice? It is necessary to tear out the heart so that the head may rise above the stars.' That voice spoke the truth, Smithers; it was the voice of my destiny.

"When the girl was lifeless, strange to say, all compassion vanished. I was once more the artist, calm and smiling; she, the model who might inspire me to herculean effort. I strode forward to where she lay in an ever-widening stain of blood and, drawing out paper and pencil, went to work in a mental daze of creation. The idiot had fled. I had nothing to disturb me—only the white snow-petals which fell softly on her upturned face and formed themselves into a spotless bandage for her severed throat. The shadows of night were gathering in before I left her. Already she was partly covered by a glistening counterpane which would hide all telltale traces by dawn.

"But now you are trembling, Smithers! Why are you trembling? Are you cold? Perhaps I had better not speak of Paul."

"Yes, tell me of Paul!" I cried in a kind of desperation. "You murderer, tell me of Paul! You killed him because you were fond of him, I presume? Oh, if my hands weren't tied!"

"Calm yourself, Smithers," Martin said. "You must hear me out before you can judge. I did not kill Paul because I was merely *fond* of him. Ah, no. You, who have shared your affections with the mob, can scarcely understand the feeling I had for *him*. He was as wife, brother and friend to me—the personification of all my earthly affection—the single link which still held me to humanity.

"From the first, I knew that this friendship was fatal to art. To develop the ego, one must travel alone. Loving hands hold us back; they seek to bind us with the ropes of affection, mercy, generosity. We must thrust them aside, we must crush them if need be, to reach our goal. All tender emotions clog the stream of inspiration. I could only create by forming myself into a machine devoid of all the warmer instincts of nature. Paul must go!

"But I was weak. I lacked the resolution to leave him. I dodged the issue. Why could I not follow my career and still keep this single affection, I asked myself. Surely it was possible. Before now many a man had led a double life. Art would not demand a complete excommunication from my fellows. As long as Paul remained, I would never be quite alone.

"Thinking that I could serve two masters at once, I engaged lodgings on Tyndall Place and soon was on intimate terms with the scrapings of the neighborhood—men who would slice a throat for slight compensation and often for the merest whim. Before many weeks had passed, I gathered about me a band of the most bloodthirsty rascals unhung. They nicknamed me 'The Boss' and were overjoyed to have a leader who could plan their little escapades skillfully and who sought no material gain for himself.

"Under my leadership a dozen murders were perpetrated and the police in every case failed to apprehend the assassin. I witnessed all of these crimes and they are reported faithfully in my first book. Yet each murder was a torture to me; and the remorse I felt when I visited Paul, was almost more than I could bear. You scarcely realized my true emotions, Smithers, on the night when we met on Tyndall Place. No doubt you thought I was calm and collected; but, in reality, I was suffering far more than you. Every blow which descended on that writhing body, fell on my soul as well. As never before, Paul's influence was about to gain the ascendancy. For one mad moment I was tempted to throw myself beneath that shower of clubs and perish with my victim.

"Although 'Many Murders' was acclaimed a great success by the leading critics, it was in reality a miserable failure. I had succeeded in writing several vivid descriptions of violent death, but they were written from the standpoint of the spectator. I had only succeeded in portraying the sensations of an eyewitness—the commonplace form of narration in horror writing. Surely there was room for great improvement in my next book. Could I not probe far deeper into the subject? Now, if I could describe accurately and vividly the thoughts and sensations of the assassin as he struck the fatal blow, I would be accomplishing a unique effect in literature. But, unfortunately, l was not blessed with an imagination. In order to write a series of such stories, I must first commit a series of such crimes. I could no longer depend on my band of cutthroats to create models for me; I must shed human blood with my own hands. Who could know the sensations of the assassin but the assassin? It was necessary for me to become an actual murderer.

"Several days after I had come to this decision, I attempted to kill a man. He had been drugged and was lying unconscious in my crime studio on Tyndall Place. I was alone with him. Stealing up beside the bed where he lay, I poised a needle-pointed stiletto above his heart. A single movement of my arm and he would have been a corpse; yet, try as I would, this simple act was beyond me. Thinking that I saw a resemblance to Paul on his white, upturned face, I sank to my knees and burst out into uncontrollable sobs. Defeated, broken, I crouched there until my intended victim awoke.

"That night I fought a great and final battle. All through the dark hours the struggle raged. At one moment my love for Paul, and all the human weaknesses which followed in its train, would gain the ascendancy; at the next, the calm and radiant goddess, Art, would hold my will in the hollow of her hand. It was not until the gray light of dawn descended on the city that the victory was won.

"'I must sever the last link which holds me to humanity,' I told myself. 'Paul must be sacrificed, as others have been sacrificed, on the funeral pyre of genius. Brave men have starved for it, shall *I* turn back? Kind men have forfeited their loved ones for it, shall *I* be weak? No, Paul, my dear friend, you must die!'"

XXI

Martin paused and passed his hand across his forehead. Great drops of perspiration had formed there, which at any moment threatened to run down into his eyes. Evidently the memory of these mental sufferings could still move him. I might have pitied the man, had I not had such a hearty detestation and horror of him.

"Three weeks later Paul and I went to the woods together," he continued. "I had shipped a barrel of whisky to the camp several days before. It was child's play for me to overcome your brother's scruples and start him drinking again. For five days I kept him in a drunken stupor by passing him my flask when he showed signs of returning to reason. On the sixth day I hid the barrel in the spring and refused to give him any more whisky. When he came to himself, he had an attack of violent melancholia. Sick in body, he was sicker yet in mind.

"As you know, Paul's fits of mental depression were rather dangerous. Before this he had always had some one

to cheer him up, some one to drag him bodily out of the
slough of despondency. But now I did just the opposite.
Instead of trying to lighten his mind, I burdened it with all
the weary weight of remorse. I gave him no hope to cling
to. I told him that what had happened here in the woods
would happen again and again; that there was no hope of
ultimate cure for a drunkard; that he was predestined to
die with *delirium tremens*. I even described his death rather
vividly. I had always had a mental ascendancy over Paul;
now I used this ascendancy as a weapon to destroy him.
When I left him by the camp fire that night, I knew that the
thought of immediate suicide was implanted in his whisky-
soaked brain.

"But how I suffered as I lay in the dark cabin waiting
for the end! All my other sufferings were as nothing
compared to this. When I finally saw his hand slide silently
in through the doorway and clutch the barrel of a shotgun
which stood against the wall, I seized the sides of my bunk
and literally held myself down. 'Only a moment now,' I told
myself. 'Only a moment!'

"And then, when I heard the loud report of the gun,
something seemed to snap in my brain—some chord of
feeling which, having parted, left me as cold as ice. Since
that day I have felt nothing—neither love nor pity, fear nor
hate. Strange, isn't it, Smithers? What was it that died with
Paul? Whatever it was, it left me free to go my own way."

"Your way shall lead to the gallows if I once get out of
here alive!" I cried defiantly. "You'd better murder me now
and have done with it!"

"I doubt if the courts would hold me responsible
for your brother's death," he said quite calmly. "Crimes
committed by the mind are beyond the reach of the law.

However, hear me out, Smithers, and you'll have iron-bound proof.

"After Paul's death, I began creating material for my new book. Patiently, cleverly, I arranged a murder in which I played the chief role and did the actual killing with my own hand. I committed that crime, calmly, coolly, without the slightest compunction. The description of it appeared in 'The Confessions of Constantine.' That book, if you remember, described my sensations—the sensations of the murderer—in the most minute and realistic fashion.

"During the next three days I committed twelve murders in all. I limited myself to that number because I was not actuated by a love for shedding blood alone. Ah, no, I destroyed life merely for art's sake. And I naturally refrained from wholesale slaughter, as I feared that my sensations would soon become dulled by overusage and that I would no longer be able to record them so vividly and with such artistic feeling. In a word, I fostered my talent.

"Soon after 'The Confessions of Constantine' was published, I began to read the papers with avidity. But I never turned to the literary sheet—the book reviews. I was tired of words; I wanted deeds. And I was not disappointed, as you know. 'The Confessions of Constantine' passed the supreme test; it was responsible for a wave of crime that swept the country from end to end. This was a triumph for art. I not only appealed to the minds of my readers; I conquered their minds. I was the maker of men's destinies, the angel of death.

"What exultation filled me during those few short months when 'The Confessions of Constantine' wandered through the world and whispered its red secrets to all mankind! How I gloated over this signal victory—a victory which no other artist had accomplished. Surely I was destined to dwell forever on the sunlit heights of great achievement. And then, just as the world seemed mine to play with at will, the roof of the heavens fell on my proudly lifted head. You know what happened, Smithers. 'The Confessions of Constantine' was condemned by the government!

"I made inquiries and soon learned who was responsible for my downfall. I did not underestimate Wilbur Huntington for an instant. The man was a brilliant psychologist and capable of doing big things as a criminal expert. He had already traced the crime-wave to 'The Confessions of Constantine,' would he not soon compare it with 'Many Murders' and make some startling deduction? Suppose he should learn that I had no imagination? Would I be safe?

"Thoughts such as these, prompted me to write that letter which he received in your studio. Before he came that night, I made my preparations. Securing the services of three murderers who could be relied upon, I hid them behind the portières in my apartment. No sooner was he well inside, before they leaped upon him and pinioned his arms behind his back. He was helpless.

"'So you decided to get me out of the way, Martin,' he said with surprising calmness. 'I thought it might come to this.'

"In spite of the great wrong the man had done me, I could not help showing him a certain amount of respect. There he stood, with a boyish smile on his face, while those assassins were nearly tearing his arms out of their sockets. He seemed as careless to pain as he was to death. Your friend cut an heroic figure, Smithers.

"'You are quick to see the truth,' I said. 'If you wished to live, you should not have treated a great book in such a manner. It may be years before I can write another equally as good.'

"'That's what I came to see you about—your art!' he cried with strange enthusiasm. 'You're going to kill me immediately, I presume?'

"'Most certainly,' I answered. 'I never waste time when I am anxious to be at work.'

"'Then hear me first,' he broke in excitedly. 'I want to speak of your work.'

"'Well?' I asked.

"'You have described crime from the standpoint of the onlooker and from the standpoint of the assassin,' he said. 'That is true, is it not?'

"'Yes,' I assented.

"'But you have missed the great situation—the truly artistic situation!' he continued quickly.

"'How so?' I demanded hotly.

"'Why, you have never written a story from the standpoint of the victim!' he cried. 'In other words, what is the exact sensation of death?'

"'What is the exact sensation of death?' I repeated dully,

"'To be sure!' he shouted almost gleefully. 'You're worse than a failure, Martin, for you are only a partial success! *You*, whom they call the recorder of sensations, have missed the only unknown sensation—that mysterious sensation of death! *There* is material beyond your reach. Till you have mastered it, you will remain a living lie. I will know that secret, but it will not be mirrored in my dead eyes! You will have to go further, Martin—further!'

"And then, Smithers, the truth of his words flashed through my brain like lightning. What *was* the sensation of death? All my life I had been straining toward that unknown knowledge without realizing it; all my life I had known instinctively that dead things guard a precious secret. Without this secret, I was a mere scribbler forced to give shopworn offerings to the muse. What *was* the sensation of death? If I knew that, unborn millions would live to fear me; my shadow would rest like black plumage over the world; and life, once gay and carefree, would shudder on the brink of the tomb!

"But now red rage flamed up in me—blind rage at my own impotence. How I hated this man who had pointed out the truth! My only thought was to destroy that brain which had grappled and was grappling with mine.

"Grasping the heavy poker which leaned against the grate, I struck him on the head with all my might. The iron bit into his skull and he fell senseless at my feet. But blind fury still possessed me. I struck again and again till his face was beaten into an unrecognizable mass.

"And then I stopped, ashamed. I knew that he had escaped; that my first blow had opened the door for him; that he was now safe from me, quite safe and the possessor of a priceless knowledge. And I dared not look into his eyes for fear that I would see that relentless question: 'What was the sensation of death?'

"You know the rest, Smithers. I dressed his body in my clothes. I slipped my ring on his finger and later that night I had him thrown into the river. Then I left the city by stealth. Solitude has always appealed to me. I took to the woods, grew a beard and soon became familiar with my new life."

He paused and regarded me solemnly for a moment. "Tell me," he muttered, "why did Huntington call me a failure? Do *you* think that I am a failure, Smithers? I have tried so hard and now—" He shook his head sadly. "We, who serve, must give everything—everything!'"

And now a new terror was added to my others. There remained no doubt in my mind. Looking up into his thin, convulsed face, I realized that Burgess Martin was mad. There he sat, his eyes fixed on mine with a speculative stare—a madman with the red stain of murder in his brain! How long before his slender, crimson finger tips would be at their wonted trade? How long had I to live?

XXII

"All that I have told you happened such a long, long time ago," Martin resumed in a weary voice. "Now nothing amuses me—nothing! For ten unbearable years that relentless question has burned my brain like molten lava. The world, no doubt, would think me mad, but the moon knows better. To-night, as I sat by the fire, she bent down from the heavens and whispered to me, telling me how I could find the answer and be as wise as she and other cold things. Just think what it must mean to be wise as the moon!

"But do not imagine that seek to learn this truth for myself alone. Ah, no, I do it for Art—I do it so that she may become all-powerful, so that she may rule over the dead as over the living. I shall leave a message behind which will open those dark portals. No longer shall the breath from the tomb be heavy-laden with mystery. The time has come for my last sacrifice!"

All this time his eyes had been fixed on me; his face had been so close to mine that I could feel his hot breath on my cheek. But now he rose and straightened himself to his full height. Slowly his right hand stole downward till it rested on the hilt of the hunting knife suspended from his belt. A moment later I saw the sharp blade gleam dully in the feeble lamplight.

"Tell me," he said softly, bending forward as a mother might stoop to caress her sleeping child. "Tell me, would you not like to go? Paul has trod that path; Huntington laughed as I struck him down. Surely *you* will not remain behind?"

And then, for the first time in all that terrible night, my courage deserted me. "Help!" I shouted. "Help!" But the moaning of the wind, that everlasting mourner, was my only answer.

"You were always a weakling," Martin said with a sneer strong in his voice. "But I will not press you. You shall be my messenger to the world."

Now he bent down lower still, and, with the speed of lightning, passed the sharp blade of the hunting knife across the arteries in his left wrist. Instantly a warm stream of blood fell on my upturned face. At this new horror, everything grew black before my eyes. I fainted.

When I regained consciousness, Martin still lived, although his blood was dry on my cheek. He sat beside the table in the center of the room, bending over it and writing hurriedly. His left arm hung motionless by his side. From the wrist a dark ribbon of blood stole downward over the hand and, separating at each finger, dripped to the floor. The storm had died down, the rain had ceased. I could distinctly hear the scratching sound his pencil made while traveling over the paper, the intermittent pattering of blooddrops on the loose boards at his feet.

For the moment I was incapable of thought. I stared stupidly at this absorbed figure, scarcely realizing the struggle going on between mind and body, between life and death. And then the pencil—that swiftly moving pencil riveted my gaze. I felt that it was being pursued, that pencil; that it was a tiny terror-stricken creature, fleeing, dodging this way and that, leaping forward in a frenzy to escape. But what pursued it? What implacable destiny waited for it silently at the end of the page? Now it faltered, now it sped on again, now it moved jerkily forward for an inch or two. And then—why, then it stopped! The race was over!

Burgess Martin sank lower and lower in his chair. The pencil slipped from his fingers to the floor. He tried to reach for it, to pick it up again; but strength was lacking. Soon his chin rested on his breast.

But how long he took to die! The lamplight was dying with him, slowly, surely, while dark shadows, clustering in the corners, grew bolder now and crept out in solemn, hovering groups. I saw them gathering about the doomed man, silently stealing forward, bending and bowing, mocking his weakness and futility of effort like evil marionettes. And once I distinctly heard a low laugh as though one were merry in the presence of death and would hide it from the world.

But now, as though spurred to final effort, Burgess Martin raised his head. He moved; he shook off death; he arose unsteadily to his feet. For an instant he stood there, grim and silent, his arms outstretched as though awaiting the cold embraces of his mistress.

"I have not the strength," he murmured. And then in a louder tone: "Forgive me if I have failed in this. I have tried so hard!

And now there came a gust of wind from the lake. It tore the blanket from the doorway. It entered. It breathed upon the lamp and there was blackness. There followed the sound of a heavy fall and then silence.

I have but little more to tell. On the following day Doctor Street arrived at Naples, and, hearing that I was in Bill Pete's cabin, hired a canoe and paddled across. He found me tied to my bunk and raving in a high fever. On the floor, within a few feet of the table, lay the stiffening remains of Burgess Martin.

Several weeks later, after I had recovered my health and strength, Dr. Street gave me further details. It seems that Martin's usually somber face was transfigured by a strange, unearthly smile and that he held in his right hand, crumpled up into a ball, a sheet of paper on which he had succeeded in writing several sentences. I have that sheet of paper before me now and, as I am convinced that his last message can do no harm in its unfinished state, I quote from it verbatim:

> I am dying, slowly, painlessly. From me are falling, one by one, the dry husks of life. A great weakness, which clarifies the senses, is stealing over me. I am a child again—a child who stands on the tiptoe of expectancy. Something is about to happen. What? I do not know. And yet I feel so sure of approaching freedom. I have lived my life behind iron bars; and now—why, now I smell the sea!

Yes, and I see it—that sea of eternity, that sea which holds a million, million souls! I hear it. My ears catch up the refrain and hold it like shells on life's shore. All my life I have sought to probe its mystery—that beautiful, sparkling sea of death.

Why am I so weak? The pencil is falling from my hand. I must hold it tighter—tighter! I have lived my life for Art's sake; I must die for Art's sake.

But hush! She is coming! My love is coming, my cold bride! And who is that beside her? Who is that who holds her hand in his? It is Death— proud Death! I behold you and I am not afraid. I will tell the world of you, Death. You cannot hide your face from me. I see the answer to my question written in your eyes. Well, l shall speak! I—

Here this strange manuscript broke off abruptly. No doubt at this moment the pencil had slipped from his hand. He had failed. But having failed, having sacrificed his life in vain, how was it that he was found with that strange, transfiguring smile on his face?

It is now five years since Martin's death. I have had plenty of time for thought. But there is a question which still puzzles me. Was he right in claiming that he had no imagination? Perhaps he had too much imagination; perhaps it was his gnawing imagination which drove him on, which turned him into a murderer and then into a madman, which finally made him cut into his own life with that sharp, inquisitive blade. Curiosity and imagination— surely they go hand in hand.

The End

About the Author

Tod Robbins (1888–1949) was born Clarence Aaron Robbins in Brooklyn to society parents and pursued both sports and poetry in his youth. When his grandfather died in 1909 Robbins inherited enough money that he didn't have to work and was able to pursue writing. He published *Mysterious Martin*, his first novel, in 1912, followed quickly by two more novels, a volume of poetry, and a number of short stories that he published in the most famous pulp magazines of the day. The most notable of these is "Spurs," a 1923 story about circus performers that would be adapted into the film *Freaks* by Tod Browning in 1932. In the early 1920s Robbins expatriated to France, where he refused to leave even at the advent of World War II and the Nazi occupation of France. As a result, he spent the majority of the war in a French internment camp. After the war, he published one final novel in 1949 and died at home in France that same year. Though Robbins' impact on the genre of horror is clear, his work has fallen mainly out of print.